The STIFF UPPER LIP

BY THE SAME AUTHOR
The Hen's House
Hush Money
The French Kiss
The Stiff Upper Lip

a novel by
PETER ISRAEL

THOMAS Y. CROWELL,
PUBLISHERS

Established 1834   New York

THE STIFF UPPER LIP. Copyright © 1978 by J. Leon Israel. All rights reserved. Printed in the United States of America. No part of this book may be used or reproduced in any manner whatsoever without written permission except in the case of brief quotations embodied in critical articles and reviews. For information address Thomas Y. Crowell, Publishers, 10 East 53rd Street, New York, N.Y. 10022. Published simultaneously in Canada by Fitzhenry & Whiteside Limited, Toronto.

FIRST EDITION

Designed by Stephanie Tevonian

Library of Congress Cataloging in Publication Data

Israel, Peter,
    The stiff upper lip.

    I. Title.
PZ4.I84St 1978 [PS3559.S74] 813'.5'4 78-3325
ISBN 0-690-01412-0

78 79 80 81 82 10 9 8 7 6 5 4 3 2 1

=1=

I didn't see her coming the first time.

It was one of those fluke-warm days Paris sometimes gets in the fall, when the jeans suits come back out of the closets and the yellowing leaves don't know which way to turn. By eleven in the morning the air was heavy with exhaust and the white sun stung your eyes even through your shades. I was headed for Le Drugstore on the Boulevard St. Germain, where they stocked my brand of pipe tobacco. I'd just bought the *Herald* at a kiosk and had turned to the Personals column on the back page when she came flying into me, full tilt.

Like I say, I didn't see her. One minute I was thinking about Bobby H.; the next I was full of hat, arms and legs, shopping bags. I did smell her, though. It was one of those expensive reeks only the alchemists at Paco Rabanne know the secret of. Then I was picking our debris off the sidewalk. One of her shopping bags said Charles Jourdan, another Dorothée Bis. A third, a tote of soft black leather, had no name at all. She too was wearing the jeans outfit, but her pants were huggers stuffed into high-heeled black boots that came up past her knees. Some white lace frilled out of the jacket collar, and a black Spanish-cowboy hat that tied under the chin topped off the effect, which was pretty stylish, if you go for the style.

"*Je vous demande pardon,*" I said, chivalrous to the end.

She took her bags from me. Dimples formed vertically in her cheeks and her teeth flashed white.

"Do you do this very often?" she said.

Her English was impeccable except for the telltale *z* sound which got into the *th*. Her tone was amused, more come-on than put-down. Before I could come up with a rejoinder, though, she'd turned and set sail up the boulevard, shopping bags swinging, the black hat tacking and luffing in the crowd.

No, I didn't follow her. The thought only crossed my mind.

The ad in the Personals column of the *Herald* read:

> **Considerable Reward** any information concerning Robert Harcourt Goldstein, 24, called "Bobby H.," last known whereabouts London July, Amsterdam-Paris August, call collect Paris 322-44-63.

It had been running all that week, and not only in the *Herald Tribune* but the Rome *Daily American*, The Athens *News*, and assorted other Old World message centers. The idea had been to blanket the continent, and if all it had produced so far were three collect calls, two of them crank and one from a Rome detective agency that offered to join the hunt, well, it was the only one that had brought any response whatsoever. The Paris sleuthery I'd subcontracted the job to had drawn a blank as well. Which was only understandable when the last known trace of Bobby H. was "Amsterdam-Paris August," but Robert Richard Goldstein, called Bobby R. to differentiate him from his son, hadn't been in an understanding mood when I'd talked to him last, which was by transatlantic hotline. Bobby R. had wanted results on Bobby H., not explanations, and he'd wanted it for about a hundred dollars' worth of tirade. Maybe that's the way it is, being a father, when you suddenly wake up to the fact that your number-one son and heir went out to lunch a couple of months ago and never came back.

I filed the *Herald* in the slit of a trash bin and went into Le Drugstore, where I joined the queue at the tobacco counter.

"Euh-rhan-morh," I said when I got to the head of the line, this being how you handle "Erinmore" in French. "*Deux, s'il vous plaît.*"

The girl at the counter reached behind her for two fifty-gram tins. I also ordered up a carton of box matches. The girl at the counter did the addition and I reached into my jacket pocket for my wallet.

And came away empty-handed.

I checked the rest of my pockets. Nothing. I checked the morning in my mind: bath, shave, dressing, breakfast in the hotel garden. In between *dressing* and *breakfast,* I remembered picking the wallet up, plus car keys, loose change, fresh handkerchief. The keys, change, and handkerchief were still there. But not the wallet. God damn.

"*Je vous demande pardon,*" I said, for the second time that morning. The girl behind the counter flashed me a short but contemptuous look, then put her hand out over the tobacco tins and turned to the next customer.

"May I, Mr. Cage?" A long jean-sleeved hand reached elegantly in front of me, a hundred-franc note folded between the index and middle fingers.

I caught a gust of Paco Rabanne.

Undoubtedly the hundred francs belonged to me too, because she was holding out my wallet in her other hand.

"Do you do this very often?" I said. "I mean, picking pockets?"

This was across the boulevard at the Café Flore. We'd gone inside to escape the pollution on the terrace. It was cool and empty inside except for a few regulars reading the newspapers over their coffees, and she ordered a kir, which to my mind is a hell of a way to treat white wine, and I my usual Glenfiddich.

"Whenever I need to," she replied.

"For pin money?" I said, gesturing at her outfit.

"No, not for the money. Only when I need to impress someone."

"Well, if you ask me, it's a hell of a strange way to impress people."

"Perhaps that depends on whom you're trying to impress, Mr. Cage."

"Oh," I said.

Our drinks came and she watched me over the rim of her glass while she sipped. I watched her back. She'd pushed the hat back onto her neck, revealing a goodly mass of light-brown hair, all of which was upswept except for two ringlets which descended by her ears, as if by accident. Only the ringlets weren't an accident. I don't suppose anything about her was. She was made up in that careful no-make-up way, except for the slash of red across her mouth and some subtler fancywork around the eyes. And younger than I'd have thought, now that I had a good look. And, much as I dislike the distinction, there was something markedly upper-crust about her, in the voice tone, the firm set of her chin, and that general pardon-my-glove confidence that comes only from generations of looking down at the rest of us mortals.

"O.K.," I conceded. "Say I'm impressed. Now what can I do for you?"

"You can hire me."

"Do *what?*" I said. It had come out perfectly matter-of-fact, like she was asking me for a match.

"That's right. Hire me. I'm looking for a job."

"Well, Miss... Miss..."

"Merchadier."

"Well, Miss Merchadier, I'm sorry, but I've got no room on my staff for another pickpocket."

She laughed at that, complete with the vertical slit-dimples and the white rows of teeth.

"Oh," she said then, smiling at me quickly, "I have other talents too."

"I'm sure you do, Miss Merchadier, but..."

"Valérie," she said. "My friends call me Val."

"All right, Valérie. But there are dozens of outfits in my business in Paris. Why me?"

"Because I picked you."

"If you did, then you got some wrong information about me. As far as my operation's concerned, two's a crowd."

This was true enough. For better or worse, the closest I'd ever come to employing anybody was an answering service, and that was several seasons back in Santa Monica, California. It turned out she knew all about Santa Monica, California. She also knew about a lot of things since, some of them none too savory. I didn't like that overly. In fact, it annoyed me no end: the idea of somebody doing that complete a job on me without my spotting him. All right: without my spotting *her*.

"That's where you're wrong, Mr. Cage. Maybe it made sense in America to operate on your own. Though I wonder. But in Paris it's outmoded and foolish. You need organization in Paris, organization and connections. With them, you can accomplish wonders. Without them...? Look at it this way: even the Lone Ranger had... had... what was his name, the Indian?"

"Tonto," I said.

"Tonto."

I didn't like, either, listening to people telling me what was wrong with my *modus vivendi*.

"I'm sorry," I said, "but I'm not the Lone Ranger and I don't need a Tonto. I'm happy with things the way they are."

"Sure," she said mockingly, "running a lost-and-found service for overfed Americans."

I'd never laid eyes on my latest client myself. Maybe Robert Richard Goldstein had a weight problem at that. Else she was talking about Americans generically.

She reached down into her black leather tote and pulled out a copy of the *Herald*. It was folded down to the classifieds on the back page, and one of them was circled in black ink. She dropped the paper onto the table.

"Once upon a time," she said, "you would have found him in your lunch hour. Now you're reduced to running advertisements and splitting your fee with other people. This is Paris, Mr. Cage, over here you're like a fish out of water. What's more, the police have their hooks into you, and, as I understand it, if you're not a good boy they're perfectly capable of throwing you back where you came from."

This too was true enough, as far as it went, but it was scarcely common knowledge. I liked to think I had a hook back into the French Law, that it was a stand-off, but it was also true that the scrape she'd referred to had been an ugly one, and that I'd come out of it with only my skin. And true, finally, that ever since, my bank account and my *modus vivendi* had been on something of a collision course.

None of which I enjoyed being reminded of.

"Just supposing," I said, semi-curious, "that things are as tough as you say they are. What makes you think I could pay you a living wage?"

"I told you," she retorted, "I don't need the money."

"Then why...?"

She slit her dimples at me again, then drained the last of her concoction.

"For the same reason as you, Mr. Cage. The kicks. For the money too, when it's there. But the kicks."

"You mean you'd do it for free if need be?"

"I didn't say that. Not at all. But I'd work for a percentage."

"A percentage of what?"

"Of our profits."

A part of me hated to disappoint the lady, but only a small part. I scraped my chair back.

"I've a feeling you've got a pretty wrong idea of what my line involves," I began. "But in any case, I've no need of..."

What she did then, though, stopped me in mid-sentence. There wasn't much to it—she just narrowed her eyes a little, fixing me with them, and at the same time licked her tongue across her upper lip—but there was no mistaking her meaning.

"As I said," she added with a slight husk to her voice, "I have other talents."

"I'm sure you do," I said, repeating myself too. "But I'm not interested."

Her lips went tight then and her head back, like she'd just been slapped. Apparently Valérie Merchadier wasn't used to being turned down.

"No," she snapped scornfully, "you're not interested. Not when you have all your airline hostesses to play with."

In this detail, though, her research was a little behind the times. The fact was that since the ugly episode I've referred to, I'd pretty much taken to going to bed alone nights.

I stood up and reached inside my jacket for my wallet, a little startled to find that it was there again.

She didn't move.

"You mean you're not even going to offer me another drink?" she asked, looking up at me.

"No."

"All right!" she said angrily. She picked up the *Herald* and brandished it at me. "What do I have to do to prove myself to you? Do you want me to find him for you? Robert Harcourt Whatever-His-Name-Is? Will that do, *Mr. Benjamin Franklin Cage?*"

This was the last surprise in her tote bag, but it packed quite a wallop. "B.F." is as far as most people have ever gotten in deciphering my name.

"Could you manage it in your lunch hour?" I said, playing for laughs, but not, to judge, with much success.

"Forty-eight hours," she replied tartly. "If I produce him within forty-eight hours, will you hire me?"

I didn't answer. Instead I slipped a fifty-franc note under my Glenfiddich glass and ran for my life.

I can't say I spent the next two days waiting for her to show. Still, some of what she'd said had struck a nerve. Fact: my dice *had* gone cold. If I'd come to Paris on a fluke, more or less, nobody (fact) had forced me to stay. Fact: I liked the place, mostly, only (fact) it had proved tough to crack in my particular specialty, which has to do, broadly speaking, with the gathering and suppression of information. Not that Paris is any less needful of services such as mine. On the contrary, the fix is in here like nowhere I've ever been. But the French have their own way of washing their dirty laundry and that includes keeping outsiders away from the bidet. Which (fact) had reduced me momentarily to certain stopgap measures, like running a lost-and-found for Americans, over- and underfed.

The rub was that "momentarily" has a way of becoming "indefinitely" without your noticing it.

So?

So I noticed it.

I did some busy-work on the Bobby H. affair. Bobby R. wanted the Law kept out of it—apparently his number-one son and heir had a history—but I did some discreet questioning in that direction. I renewed the want-ad for another week. I called the detective agency I'd retained and gave them a pep talk.

All of which I expected would produce nothing. In this I wasn't disappointed.

Oh yes, and one night I got laid. And (fact), in her spare time she did work for Air France.

The voice didn't bother introducing itself on the phone.

"Are you going to be there for another hour?" she said.

Maybe a part of me had been waiting for her at that. And maybe another part of me was relieved that she'd missed her two-day deadline. If only by half an hour or so.

"Well," I said, glancing at my watch, "it's my lunch hour, remember? I've got a lot of crimes to solve. I . . ."

"Stay where you are, Cage," she interrupted. "Just stay right there."

I started to answer, but the line was already dead.

An hour later, give or take a few minutes, the phone rang again. It was the desk clerk. He sounded a little doubtful about it, but I had two visitors, was it all right to send them up?

Yes, I said, it was all right to send them up.

She'd changed for the occasion, and I could see why the clerk had hesitated. The hat was gone and her hair hung lank to her shoulder blades. She wasn't wearing any make-up, not that that did her any harm, but her jeans looked like they'd been chewed dry. She had on an equally wrinkled work shirt that was unbuttoned to the navel and over it one of those scraggly skin vests of dubious, if animal, origin. The boots had given way to a pair of scuffed black clogs. All that remained from her Café Flore outfit was the black tote, but it too had been knocked around to fit the costume.

The young man with her was of a piece. Allowing for the fact that his hair had thatched out and that he needed a shave, he fit the description I'd had pretty well. He was a tall, skinny kid with freckles and glasses and tired eyes. He wore a pair of rubber sandals that might have once belonged to Michelin radials, jeans, and a neckless baseball shirt with UCLA on it. Put the two of them together and they could have passed for just another couple in that international youth fauna that crawls around under the Paris cobblestones.

"Mr. Cage," Valérie said while I closed the door behind them, "Mr. Goldstein."

We didn't shake hands. Bobby H. slumped into a chair without an invitation. Valérie stayed on her feet.

"Bobby," she said, looking down at him, and though she was in profile I could see her bite her upper lip a second before continuing, "I hate to break the news to you this way, but Mr. Cage was hired to find you. By your old man."

The message didn't seem to register. She repeated it. He glanced up at me, then at her. Uncomprehending, then comprehending. Whatever she'd told him, it clearly hadn't been that. He squinted. Then he took off his glasses, closed his eyes, and rubbed at them with his fingers. Then he started to laugh, still rubbing. Then he stopped laughing.

"No shit," he said. He gazed up at her, shaking his head.

"I'm sorry, Bobby," she said, "but that's how it is."

He looked at me again, like he was seeing me for the first time. Maybe he was measuring his chances. In any case, he put his glasses on again, then sank back into the chair. And laughed again. And stopped laughing again.

"You cunt," he said to Valérie, shaking his head again.

I expected some kind of plea, but I didn't get it.

"O.K.," he said to me flatly. "Like you've found me. So what do we do now?"

"Now we call your old man," I said.

"And then what?"

"That's up to him." I glanced at my watch. "The only trouble is: it's a little early, with the time change."

"What time is it?"

"In Connecticut? About six forty-five in the morning."

"Oh, that's not too early, you know? He'll be up. He wouldn't miss the seven-twenty train, not in a blizzard. He'll be drinking his cocoa now. Would you believe that? His stomach can't take coffee in the morning. Well, go ahead, then. Call him."

He gave me the number for good measure.

My telephone is on an end table just past the couch. I went over to it and sat down.

"What are you?" said Bobby H. "Some kind of private eye?"

"More or less."

"What they call a shamus?"

"They used to."

"Then tell me one thing. How much is he paying you?"

It wasn't any of his business what I was getting paid. On the other hand, I thought it might do him some good to find out what he was worth, if only to his father.

I told him.

"The cheap mother," he said. He repeated the figure, sneered at it. "I'll tell you what, Mr. . . . Excuse me, what did you say your name was?"

"Cage," I said.

"I'll tell you what, Cage," he said, grinning at me suddenly. "What would you do if I doubled it?"

"And paid me in what?" I asked. "Brown sugar?"

"Brown sugar" is what they call the happy dust they're peddling these days on the street corners of Europe.

"Like whatever you want," said Bobby H. coolly.

I thought about it, but not for very long.

"One client per family," I said, picking the receiver off the hook.

"Put it down, Cage," Valérie said.

"*Oui, Monsieur?*" the hotel operator was saying.

"I want to call overseas, to the U.S.A. The number's..."

"I said put the phone down, Cage. *Now!*"

For the past minute or so, I'd let Valérie out of my sight. I'd made the same kind of mistake before. Now I turned toward her. God knows what else she carried in the black tote, but now she had a miniature and snub-nosed popgun in her hand. It was pointed at me. It didn't look very serious. On the other hand, *she* did.

I glanced at Bobby H. He didn't seem to know any more about what was going on than I did.

"Of all the goddam things," I said, or some such immortal remark.

"*J'écoute, Monsieur,*" said the hotel operator in my ear.

"Never mind," I told her, "I'll call back later," and hung up the phone.

I sat there a minute. Nobody moved. Then I stood up.

"All right," I said to Valérie, "suppose you put away the popgun and tell us what the hell this is all about."

"I'm good with popguns," she said to me levelly. "You take another step and I'll have to put a hole through your kneecap. Now stand where you are. You, Bobby," she ordered, not taking her eyes off me. "Search him."

"But I thought..."

"I said *search* him!"

Bobby H. came up behind me and went through my pockets, tossing the items he found on the couch. If I'd had a switchblade hidden in my rectum he wouldn't have found it, but otherwise he did a pretty creditable job.

Anyway, I don't own a switchblade.

"No weapons," he said when he was done. "Not much of anything, you know?"

"Bring me his wallet."

This was getting to be a habit. Bobby H. took my wallet over to her. She went through it, leaving everything but the cash. This she held out in a wad to him.

"Here, take it," she said. "Count it."

He did. It came to a little over a thousand francs.

"Take it if you want," she said. "It'll pay for your time."

"But I thought..."

"I said take it," she repeated peremptorily. "Then split. I'll hold him here for half an hour. Then you're on your own."

He stuffed the money into a jeans pocket.

"But listen, Val, don't you want me to..."

"Half an hour," she repeated. "Don't ask questions. I'll explain it later. Just split!"

And so he split, did Bobby H.

She waited, listening, until the elevator door opened and shut in the hallway. Then she walked slowly across the space between us, stopping a step in front of me.

The popgun was still pointed at my chest, but I saw the vertical creases on either side of her mouth.

"How am I doing," she said softly.

"Not bad for a beginner," I said, but..."

She closed the remaining space between us. The popgun lowered as she came, and then I couldn't see it any more. She put her arms around my neck. She went up on tiptoe, her body climbing up mine, and she kissed me slowly, tonguing, like time had gone out of style.

Not bad for a beginner.

Later on, I asked her how she'd found Bobby H. This brought out the even white teeth as well as the vertical dimples, and the skin crinkled seductively around her eyes.

"Secrets of the profession," she said.

"*Touché*," I said. "But why bring him up here if you were going to let him go?"

"I didn't know that ahead of time. It only occurred to me once we were here."

"What changed your mind?"

"You both did."

I didn't get it. She didn't strike me as the type to have gone soft on Bobby H.

"Didn't he offer you double what his father had?" she said.

"That's right."

"And you turned him down. Were you just being moral? Or was it that the price wasn't high enough? Supposing, though, that we let him go and the double became triple. Or more."

"What makes you think that? What makes you think he won't just disappear again."

"He can't."

"Why not?"

"For one thing, he's making too much money."

I'd been right about that, as it turned out. Bobby H. was aptly named, even if the sugar trade wasn't really his action.

"That's for one thing," I said. "What else?"

"Well, for another," she said, smiling up at me, "he thinks he's in love with me."

But later still she said: "Now let's talk terms."

She was sitting up in bed, smoking a cigarette, the sheet pulled up to her waist and the sweat drying on her breasts.

"What terms?" I said, stoking my pipe.

"The terms of my employment. We agreed that if I delivered Bobby to you, you'd hire me."

"I agreed to no such thing. Besides, I seem to remember that you undelivered him."

She eyed me sexily.

"Oh, come on, Cage, stop being so tough and intractable and hard to get."

I eyed her in return, not to be tough and intractable, but because something had just struck me, call it an insight, and I was looking for corroboration.

"Look," I said. "You've put on quite a show. The best. But you can't tell me you went to all that trouble just to get a job."

She sighed.

I lit a match, lit the pipe, shook the match out.

"How did you guess?" she said quietly.

"Secrets of the profession," I replied. "But maybe you'd better tell me the rest of it."

"O.K.," she said, her eyes holding mine. "The rest of it is that I want you to keep someone I know from getting killed."

=2=

I'm trying to think of an American equivalent. It was a little like running into a skirt in Los Angeles who was freaked out on bicycle racing. And not Tour de France bicycle racing either. More like the Tour de Rhode Island. Imagine, if you can, a red-blooded, liberated American female who couldn't tell Kareem Abdul Jabbar from Doctor J. but could rattle off the first ten finishers in last summer's Tour de Rhode Island.

It was a little like that.

I bet you didn't even know they played *le basket* in France, much less in a pro league. That's right, I'm talking about the round-ball game on the hardwood floor, the one where you try to throw the ball through a hoop without stepping on anybody's knuckles. Up to a few years ago, not many Frenchmen knew more about it than that, and the guys who played it were bakers and paperhangers by trade, and drove their own cars to bandbox gyms, and passed the hat at half time. To give you an idea, the so-called "Champion of France," year-in year-out, was Villeurbanne, and the closest the game ever got to Paris was the working-class suburb of Bagnolet.

Don't ask me where Villeurbanne is.

But Valérie sure could tell you.

Anyway, times have changed in *le basket français*. They've got hot water in the showers now, and the teams travel by train and plane, and the pay can go as high as 10,000 francs a month, which is 2,000 U.S. greenbacks, plus bonuses if you make the European play-offs. There's even a vocabulary to go with it, like *lancer-franc* for free throw and *le smash* for slam-dunk, and the sports pages print the standings, and on the odd weekend afternoon, when there's nothing else going on, you can even catch a game on the tube. And all this because, a few years ago, some far-sighted promoter got the idea of opening the French game to foreigners. Right now the limit is two to a club, plus however many can get themselves naturalized, and I'll give you one guess where they come from and what color they are.

Turn it around the other way.

Say you're a kinky-haired black kid growing up in the slums of L.A. As long as you can remember, you've had a basketball in your hands, and you could dribble behind your back before you could spell your name. You played junior-high ball and playground ball and you made All-City in high school and they even paid you to go play in college. All along people have been telling you the round ball is your ticket out, look at Wilt, man, look at Jabbar, look at Sy Wicks and Curtis Rowe. Hey, look at them. Only it hasn't panned out that way for you. Maybe your college club doesn't make the tournaments. Or the night the scouts come to look you over, you shoot one for eleven. Or maybe it's simple statistics. Like there are how many thousands playing college ball in America? And how many make the pro league? A couple of hundred, no more.

So you've been had, right? Right in the American Dream, Spade Department. Well, you aren't the first one.

Only then, one day, the Man comes to talk. You've never seen him before, but he's the Man all right, even though he talks with a crazy accent. He's seen you play, and he likes what he's seen. He even has a plane ticket for you, made out in your name, one way to Paris, France, and a cash bonus if you use it. Shit, man, Pa-*ree!* So you're not pulling down two thou a month, more like a hundred bucks a game plus expenses, and so the Man never told you nobody'd speak your language, not even the coach, and that the French red wine'd give you the runs worse than Thunderbird. But since when did they have to *pay* you to play ball? And don't it beat unemployment?

Roscoe Hadley, though, didn't get to France that way.

The way Roscoe Hadley told it, he was mooching down the street one day on the outskirts of Paris, minding his mutton chops, when he heard this noise coming from a building. A funny thump-thump noise, and familiar, kind of. He walked in. Sure enough, it was a gym. A bunch of French cats were shooting baskets, in this gym, on the outskirts of Paris. And Roscoe's palms started to itch. He took off his jacket. He took off his shoes so as not to mark the floor. He picked up a loose ball, palmed it. Then he showed them a trick or two, like Roscoe's finger-roll. Then they did a little one-on-one; then two-on-one; then three-on-one; then the whole *she*-bang trying to take the ball away from Roscoe.

And what happened then?

"Well," said Roscoe Hadley, "What happ'n then just happ'n, man. Natchr'l. It was workin' the kinks out. That an' finding me a pair o' shooze."

At that, his version was probably pretty accurate. Allowing for an omission or two.

Between that day in the gym and the night, almost a year later, when we drove down to see him play, there'd been a lot of changes. And not only for Roscoe. The French pro league, you see, has a First Division of sixteen teams. At the end of each season, the bottom three teams in the standings drop into the Second Division and the top three from the Second move up. When Roscoe started playing for his club, they were somewhere in the middle of Second Division limbo; by the summer, they were on their way up to basketball heaven. Then, over the summer break, the club owner got carried away. First he moved the team from the Paris suburbs to a so-called "new city" some forty kilometers south on the autoroute. Then he hired his second foreigner, a balding black rebounder from Oakland, by way of Barcelona and Milan, called Odessa Grimes.

Or "Greemse," in French.

Oh yes, and in the meantime Roscoe Hadley had met Valérie. And fallen in love.

The night we saw him play, we missed the first ten minutes trying to find the joint. Valérie had been there before, but it wasn't hard to get lost. The autoroute off-ramp took us onto a loop which circled the new city, but whenever we followed the "Palais des Sports" signs off the loop, a forest of skyscraper dormitories closed in on us, and the only way out of the forest was back onto the loop. Finally we parked and hiked our way in through a futuristic shopping-mall labyrinth. It was the sound that guided us the last kilometer, a steady two-syllable chant that went "AD-LAY AD-LAY AD-LAY AD-LAY" and meant, allowing for the French inability to handle the English H, that Roscoe Hadley was doing his thing.

That "Palais des Sports," stuck in the middle of a shopping center some forty kilometers from Paris, was a little concrete-domed gem of an arena, with a seating capacity of some 5,000 including laps, and it was full to bursting. Maybe *le basket* hasn't caught on yet in the capital, but out there in the boondocks of the twenty-first century, where the only competition for the entertainment franc is the tube, Roscoe's show had them stomping in the aisles.

And pretty exciting stuff, if you didn't know any better. Even if you did. The game itself was really two games, one involving four black American giants and the other half a dozen sawed-off Frenchmen who, to judge from the rare moments they touched it, still thought a round ball was something you dribbled with your feet. The match-ups in the two-on-two, though, were pretty unequal, and not only because of Roscoe Hadley. Odessa Grimes was a monumental slab of glistening black granite who looked like he should have been holding up a building instead of two-stepping around a basketball court. He was the kind of player you never notice much until the other team misses a shot, which in this case was often. Call it intimidation, and Odessa Grimes knew how to intimidate. Because whenever the ball came off the hoop, up would go Odessa, bald head and all, crashing the boards like he was going to eat them, the rim and the net too, plus anything that got in his way, man or beast. And down, the ball in his paws, and up, with a flick of the wrists, to fling it out to mid-court, where Roscoe was already breezing in high. A couple of dribbles later, Roscoe would hit the foul line, and then he'd take off. A feint, a twist, a head fake or two—all in mid-air—and then he'd be floating at the hoop, hairdo and all, and it was two more points and "AD-LAY AD-LAY AD-LAY."

Only the referees kept the rout from becoming a stampede. They were French, of course; so was Descartes. According to Descartes' way of looking at reality, anything that goes up has got to come down, meaning that there was no way you could do what Roscoe did without cheating. Descartes, I guess, never heard of Elgin Baylor and body control, and neither had the French referees. So they called Roscoe for traveling even though his feet never touched the floor, and for charging, goal-tending, grab-assing, and assorted other infractions they thought up on the spot, and the crowd threatened mayhem, which turned into a standing ovation when Roscoe came out with four fouls and a twenty-point lead shortly before half time, followed by another standing ovation when the lead dwindled in the second half and he had to come back on, and when he quit for good, with forty-two points and leaving Odessa Grimes to mop up, you'd have sworn you were in the L.A. Forum and that Baylor, West, and Co. had just put away the Knicks in the seventh game of the finals.

"Just like the good old days," I said.

"That's the trouble," said Valérie, biting her nails.

They came out of the arena together, four jolly black giants in blazers and gray flannels. They'd driven down from Paris together, and apparently they did pretty much everything together when the schedules allowed, along with the other brothers who played the European circuits. They came clowning and hotdogging through an admiring crowd like all four of them had won the game. Until, that is, they saw us waiting for them. Then the grins wiped off their faces like erasers sweeping a blackboard. This wasn't because of Valérie. They could tolerate a white French chick. But I, to judge, was a real conversation-stopper.

Valérie introduced me around. Nobody shook my hand, though, and when Roscoe allowed as how he was going with us, he had to go palaver with them, and it took the whole tribal bit, complete with palm slaps and hey-babies, to keep them from coming along to chaperone him.

As is, we had enough trouble fitting him in. I still drive the Giulia, which is a normal-sized car for normal-sized people, but not for somebody who goes six-seven without his afro and whose hands hang down to around his knees. We tried him out in the front, but there was no way, and finally we had to settle for the bottom half of him in the back and the rest draped forward between the bucket seats.

Don't get me wrong, six-seven isn't that abnormal a height and I don't want to make him out a freak. But you couldn't help think it when you saw him off the court: the arms which had no place to go but down, the watermelon hands, the long, flapping feet. He kept his eyes on his feet when he walked, like they'd go off without him if he didn't, and his body motion was all herky-jerk like his bones were attached to wires. All in all, he reminded me of one of those water birds, the ones that are all line and beauty when you see them flying but look fairly ridiculous flapping around on dry land. The more so in Ivy League blazer and flannels.

Once we got back to Paris, we took him to the Coupole on the Boulevard Montparnasse. They're open till the wee hours, and they serve a mean *côte de boeuf*, which is a beef chop for two. Roscoe had one all by himself, along with a platter of French fries, this on top of a double portion of herring in cream and a mushroom omelette, and underneath a hot-fudge sundae with toasted almonds. He ate slowly, steadily, taking his time, but all during the meal, and after, when we talked over coffee and brandy, his eyes took in the vast room and the people sitting at the tables and standing up to go and coming in the doors and going out. His hoods were down and his gaze cool, but he was looking just the same, and I don't think he'd have taken kindly to people coming up behind him.

"Ma-a-an," he said, chuckling, when he'd finished off the sundae, "one thing I sure don't miss about the U.S. of A. is the *food*. You don't have a *see*-gar by any chance?"

We ordered him a cigar. He rolled it between his fingers, smelled it, then rolled it between his lips, then lit it and puffed. I almost hated to interrupt his pleasure.

"Well, Roscoe..." I said. "If, that is, you still want me to call you Roscoe?"

I'd done my homework. I knew Roscoe Hadley hadn't always been his name.

He glanced at me, quicker with his eyes than I'd have expected.

"That's what folks call me," he said mildly.

"All right," I said. "Then suppose you tell me what the trouble is."

"The trouble?"

"From what Valérie's told me, you've got plenty of it."

"I *had* plenty of it, man. Long time ago. Nowadays my troubles are over." I didn't say anything. "Besides, man, if Val tole you all about it, what you need me for?"

"I'd like to hear your version."

"*My* version? Well, like I say, a *long* time ago I had me some trouble, yes I did. On'y I walked away from it. I kep' on walkin' an' the trouble stayed where it was. Shoot, man," he said, chuckling at the room through the cigar smoke, "you name the place an' I *been* there! Anyways, now that's over an' done wit', ole Roscoe's come home to *roos'*. Paris, France, man, that's my *home*, I don't budge."

It was nigger talk, in a heavier accent than the way I tell it, and put on, I suppose, for my benefit. Or the benefit of anybody who happened to be listening.

"And now you're playing ball again."

"Yeah, man, ain't it the greates'? You saw me tonight, man, how many I score? I got it goin' good, jus' throw me the pumpkin, man, two points fo' the *home* team."

"Too good, maybe," I said. "So good people are starting to talk about you."

"Yeah, these French folks sure do like to *talk*."

"I wasn't thinking of the French. According to what Valérie's told me, the word's gotten around, even to far-off places. Like California, for instance. Even people out in L.A. are starting to say: 'Guess who I hear's playing ball again.'"

He didn't respond. He just blew smoke into the air and chased it with a series of small rings.

"People like Johnny Vee, Roscoe?"

He didn't look at me then, but his mustache twitched.

"Johnny Who?"

"Johnny Vee. You forget, else Valérie forgot to tell you. I'm from L.A. too."

"I don' know no Johnny Vee."

This was a fairly dumb answer. It was, in fact, a fairly dumb conversation, and going nowhere. By this time Valérie was staring into her coffee cup. Roscoe's gaze was across the room. The only other person in sight that I knew was the waiter. I caught his eye and made an adding motion with my index finger. He nodded back at me.

"O.K., Roscoe," I said. "Suit yourself. But if you ever remember who Johnny Vee is and want to talk about it, you know where to get hold of me. Anyway, don't forget that it wasn't my idea to come along tonight."

"Not *your* idea!" he said, aloud. "Not *your* idea! Well, shoot, man, it sure as shit wasn't *mine!*"

Which narrowed it down, kind of. Valérie looked up at me, then at him.

Then she started to cry.

I haven't said much about her that night. Up to this point, she'd made herself scarce. Probably she'd had it in mind for me to take over; but there was also something equivocal about her position. I

—25—

mean, I'd asked her if she was in love with Roscoe Hadley, and she'd asked me back if I was jealous. I'd said no, I wasn't jealous, and she'd said the word *love* wasn't in her vocabulary. I'd said why had she gone to so much trouble for a stiff if she wasn't in love with him, and she'd said men didn't ask questions like that unless they were jealous, and we'd tangoed it down to the end of the ballroom and back. As far as I was concerned, though, the one time we'd gone to bed together had been by way of sealing a bargain. It had had its moments, sure; but it hadn't been repeated.

Anyway, now she was blubbering full-tilt, her shoulders aquiver, her face buried in the Coupole's napery. She pulled out all the stops, and if it was nothing more than a female trick, the tears welling out of her eyes when Roscoe pulled her hands away were the genuine article.

"Shit, Val," said Roscoe Hadley hoarsely, "I'll tell him. I'll tell him everything, honey."

He kept repeating that.

Finally she let him lift her head. He took her whole face in his palm and stared at her anxiously. The hoods had lifted and his eyes were suddenly big and serious. If she wasn't in love with him, I'd sure have to say he was with her.

Even at the risk of appearing jealous.

He sweet-talked her, and she let him. Then she went off to the toilet for repairs, looking suddenly small in a black velvet pants suit with a silk foulard spilling out of the neck. And while she was gone, and after she came back, Roscoe Hadley did tell me everything. Mostly. In fact, he was quite the raconteur. We ordered more coffee, and cognac to keep it company, and by the time he was done and had outgrabbed me for the check, they were stacking chairs on the tables around us.

Suffice it to say, for now, that the day he picked up a loose ball in that Paris gym, he became a marked man again. Maybe the "trouble," like he'd said, had stayed where it was those years when he'd been on the move under an assumed name, but once he had the ball in his hands, it was like programmed for him to start shooting hoops with it, and once that happened it was only a matter of time before somebody said: "Hey, I hear there's a boy, over in Paris, France, of all places, name of Hadley, plays just like Jimmie Cleever used to. They say he's tearing up the league." At which, six thousand miles or not, the trouble would have to go take a look. In fact, according to Roscoe, the trouble had already looked. And Roscoe, or Jimmie, had gotten the word; his buddy and teammate, Odessa Grimes, had passed it on to him.

"It sounds to me like you've got two choices," I told him when he was done.

"Yeah, me too," he said, stroking his mustache. "But look, man, I *like* it over here. I'm not runnin' no more, that's behind me. I did my time like, all those runnin' years. Now I'm playin' ball again, it's what I mean to do. The money's good. It'll be better once we win the league. Four, five, six more playin' years, more if I'm lucky. Then there's coachin'. They *needs* coachin', man. Basketball's *growin'* over here. They're even talkin' about a all-Europe league. 'Sides," he added, looking at Valérie, "there's other things keep me here."

Valérie looked at me, then away.

"Tell him to quit, Cage," she said quietly.

That was one of his choices, maybe not the best. In any case, he wasn't having any part of it.

"No way," he said, blowing smoke rings. "Let them come. I'm ready this time." Then, at me: "I'm goin' to fight them this time, Mister."

"You and what army?"

"Oh, I got friends."

"Who, Odessa?"

"Yeah, Odessa for one. He's a good ole blood, Odessa."

"That's not a choice," I said, "that's suicide. What are you going to fight them with, basketballs?"

"We can take care of ourself, man."

"Sure, you can. And they'll run you down while you're doing it. They'll run right over you and make it look like an accident. You've been away too long, Roscoe. You forget."

He shook his head slowly.

"No, I don't forget."

"Neither do they."

There was another possibility, and the only way I figured I could be of use to him.

"You can always try negotiating," I counseled Roscoe Hadley.

"Negotiatin'? Negotiatin' with what, man?"

I shrugged.

"I'm none too sure," I said. "But it's up to us to find it."

It was too late, though, too late for me and my bright ideas. Like I said, they don't forget. A couple of days later, the Paris Law had one dead black basketball player on their hands and another one they couldn't find. They found me instead. The only thing was that the dead man was Odessa Grimes, who'd been slit ear to ear, jungle-bunny style, and the one who'd disappeared was Roscoe Hadley.

=3=

"Least you were wrong about one thing," said Roscoe Hadley. He ran his hands into his hair on either side and squeezed. "They didn't make it look like no accident. They made it look like it was *me*."

"Why did they kill him, Roscoe?"

"*Why*? You ask me *why*? How the hell do *I* know, man?"

The *they* he was talking about wasn't the French press, but it could have been. Less than twenty-four hours had gone by since Odessa Grimes had been found with his throat slit in the locker room of the Paris University Club, but the French press, true to form, already had the crime solved. One newspaper, to its credit, still hesitated. The caption under Roscoe's photograph only asked the question: "Is this the assassin of the black American basketball star?" But the rest had already gone on to the motive: "Why would Roscoe Hadley have murdered his teammate?" and the Communist blatt had blamed it on the invasion of capitalist imperialism, made in U.S.A.

As far as I was concerned, the verdict was doubtful, but my stomach was still riding a trampoline. It had started jumping the day before; it hadn't stopped. Among other things, I was none too happy about the hideaway Valérie had found him. Admittedly, she hadn't had time to go house-hunting, but if you were going to try hiding a long-armed spade in Paris, one who went six-seven in his socks and had his picture in all the media, all-white Neuilly was about the last place you'd choose.

"O.K.," I said to Roscoe, "now let's go over what happened to you yesterday."

"I already tole Val, man."

The lady in question was standing by the window staring out over the rooftops toward the Bois de Boulogne and looking a little frayed around the edges.

"Right. And now you're going to tell me."

"O.K.," he said with a sigh.

"From the beginning."

"The beginning, yeah. Well, where it begins, man, is that I overslep'. I was supposed to meet some of the brothers at the Puke yesterday mornin', like we do. Odessa too. On'y I overslep'. Shit, man, there's no law against *that*, is there?"

The Puke stood for the P.U.C., or Paris University Club, which runs an indoor sports emporium up at the top of the Boulevard St. Michel. There's a nice little gym in the basement, and though you're supposed to be a member to use it, nobody I know ever got asked for his diploma.

"Who else was there," I said, "besides Odessa?"

"How do *I* know, man? I was in bed!"

"But who was supposed to be there?"

"Anybody who was in town."

"Well? Who was in town?"

"I don' know. Johnson and Bully Reed mos' likely, you saw them play the other night. Ath'ton. The boys from Bagnolet too, they's got a home game comin' up. Plus a couple o' bloods from Barcelona, tha's what Odessa said."

"Barcelona?"

—30—

"Barcelona in Spain, man."

"Isn't that a hell of a long way to come for a pick-up game?"

"They had an exhibition up in Belgium. Them an' some Belgium club. Jus' passin' through Paris. Odessa knows 'em. Leas' he did."

It still struck me as strange that pro athletes would not only play for free but go out of their way to do it. Unless, that is, they had other business in Paris. But, according to Roscoe, the class basketball in Europe went on not in the leagues but in the pick-up action at the Puke, where they had nobody to put it on for but each other and the losers paid for beers.

"O.K., so you overslept. Then what happened?"

"Then I woke up, man."

"Where?"

"In bed, where did you think?"

"And what time was that?"

"I don' know exackly. Must have been near one."

"You didn't know what time it was but you still knew you'd overslept, right?"

"Tha's right. I oversleeps a lot during the season. I needs my sleep."

He had his head down, though. His hands were into his hair again and squeezing, like he was in a big wind and holding on to his wig. I glanced at Valérie, but she was still gazing out the window, counting chimneys.

"Then what did you do?"

"I got dressed, got me a cab, rode over to the Puke."

"You didn't eat breakfast?"

"Naw. I wasn't hungry."

"Where'd you find the cab?"

"Down on Abbesses, man. You can always find a cab down on Abbesses, pretty near."

Abbesses is the name of a street in Montmartre. Roscoe Hadley lived just up the hill from it.

"So you rode over to the gym in a cab. What time'd you get there?"

"I don' know. Say half an hour in the traffic. That'd make it half pas' one maybe."

"And you thought they'd still be there?"

"Shit, man, sometimes we jus' keeps on playin'. We loses track o' time. Guys drop out, go 'round to the café, guys come back in."

"What café?"

"Any café, man. There's plenty o' cafés near the Puke."

"So what happened when you got there?"

His hands had come out of his hair for a while, to fiddle with his mustache, but now they grabbed again.

The vibes had started going bad, he said, even before he got there. He'd made the cab stop a block away. A good thing too. He saw the blue lights blinking even before he saw the cars. They were blocking half the Boulevard St. Michel, police cars, ambulances, they'd made a regular traffic jam, and a big crowd of people was jammed on the sidewalk in front of the Puke, with the police holding them back.

"I was *scared*, man. It look like all hell had bust loose. Lord, I thought, now it's started. It like to blow my mind inside out."

"What made you so scared?"

"*Shoot*, man! I figured if they got Odessa, it was my turn nex'! How'd I know they wasn't still in that crowd, waitin' fo' *me?*"

"Who's *they?*"

"Johnny Vee's boys, who else? The hit men he sent in."

"But how'd you know it was Odessa?"

"I didn't know, man! But I *knew!* We was *thick*, man, me an' Odessa. Soon as I knew they'd got some black man."

"But how'd you know they'd got anybody?"

"I ast somebody. I said, 'What's goin' on in there, man?' Then I *saw* him! I saw the stretcher come out, them loadin' him into the ambalance, saw the ambalance drivin' off, the sireen..."

"Who'd you ask?"

"*Ask?* Ask what?"

"You said you asked somebody what had happened."

"Tha's *right!* I ast somebody on the street. Somebody says, 'They killed some black man.' 'Killed who?' I says. 'Some black man,' he says."

"Did you talk to him in French?"

"French? How do I know, man? French? English? You don' understan', I was *scared!* I thought that was *me* on the stretcher! I know that sounds crazy now, but that was *me*, man! I could see *me!* I mean, maybe I had two feets on the sidewalk, but I was thinkin'... not like it *could*'ve been me but like it *was* me! Somebody's come into the Puke, man, an' sliced me ear to ear! Jus' like openin' a can o' tomatoes."

"How did you know he'd been sliced ear to ear?"

"Because that was *me* on the stretcher, man! An' I was already *dead!*"

His hands had come free, palms up and gesturing, and he was looking at me now, niggerlike, eyeballs rolling in the sockets. They left a lot of white. He sure *looked* scared. Maybe you could say his storytelling was so good that he'd spooked himself.

"So what did you do then, Roscoe? Once you were dead?"

"What'd I do? I ran, man. I took off like a big bird. Oh, like I didn't run, but I walked fast. I had to *git*, man, that was the one idea in my head. I must've been all over town, walkin', didn' know where I was goin', didn' know what I was doin', tried telephonin', telephoned you but you wasn't there, telephoned Val but Val wasn't there, man, I felt like a ghost, I don't know...."

But he couldn't remember where he'd gone. He'd felt like a ghost. He'd been in cafés and out of cafés, he couldn't remember which or where, half the cafés in Paris it seemed like. Had he had anything to eat? No, he couldn't remember eating. Maybe ghosts don't have to eat. Yes, he could remember being up on Gaïté sometime, the rue de la Gaïté, because the brothers had had the public dice game out on the sidewalk, the one where they mark off the top of a carton into a betting layout, he could remember seeing that, it must have been up on Gaïté because that's where they play it. But otherwise, nothing, until he'd gotten Valérie on the telephone finally. Yes, that had been from a café on Gaïté. When he told her what had happened, she'd told him not to move from where he was. But he'd been too scared to stay put. But no, he couldn't remember where he'd gone next.

According to Valérie, it had taken her the rest of the afternoon to find him. She'd tracked him to a bar off the avenue d'Italie, where he was already halfway up to the astral plane on Pernod and water. Then they'd driven around awhile because, ghost or not, she hadn't wanted to go to the Neuilly apartment till after dark.

The Neuilly apartment belonged to a friend of hers. The friend was out of town; the place was empty; she'd gotten the key.

That was yesterday.

This was today.

"There's one thing," I said to Roscoe. "I know ghosts don't need to, but the way you tell it, you've gone something like thirty-six hours without eating."

"Without eating? No, man, I had some stuff to eat."

"Not here anyway."

"Not here? No, not here. But when I was walkin'. I had some stuff then. Some crêpes. I had some crêpes up on Gaïté, they sell 'em on the street. Jelly an' sugar. An' some dogs. I had me a couple o' dogs in a café."

Valérie had turned around by the window and was watching us. In fact, I realized, she'd been watching us for some time, and me more than Roscoe.

"You're lying, Roscoe," she said flatly. The way she said it, you knew she wasn't talking about hotdogs either.

The thing was, I knew how *I* knew; but I didn't know how *she* did.

Roscoe glanced up at her, then away.

"Look, honey," he said, "why don' you go out awhile, take in a little air, buy us some *food?* Now we started talkin' about it, my stomach's rumblin'. I bet Cage here too, he could use..."

For once, though, his voice trailed off. It must have been her expression. Her lips were tight, her eyes narrow. Roscoe stood partway up. His king-sized palms were spread in some kind of beseeching gesture.

"Look, honey, there's something I want to talk to Cage here about. Personal-like, you know what I means?"

I began to have an idea why.

"Roscoe," I said, "there wasn't any traffic jam yesterday up on St. Michel, and no crowd of people."

"Shit, man, maybe I was wrong about the *time*." He stood up the rest of the way. "Maybe it wasn't half pas' one. I *tole*..."

"At no time, Roscoe. Not at half past one or any time. They had the ambulance on the back street. They took his body out that way. There was only one cop car you could recognize, the rest were unmarked. You..."

"What are you calling me?" he said, nostrils flaring. "A *liah?*"

"I don't think you were anywhere near the Puke yesterday. And like you said: a good thing too."

"Yeah? What makes you so sure about that?"

"Because I was there myself."

Let's get one thing out of the way right now: I didn't kill Odessa Grimes, I only found him.

I'd gone up to the P.U.C. gym myself, late that morning, looking for him and Roscoe. My California sources of information weren't what they'd once been, but I had a notion I wanted to try on them. Both together. I was late getting there, though, thanks to a transatlantic conversation, largely one-way, with one Robert Richard Goldstein, and by the time I arrived the action was fast and frantic. It was strictly playground style: no whistles, no refs, no fouls, no time-outs. And no Roscoe either. And no Odessa Grimes.

I asked around if anybody had seen them. Nobody had. I watched the action for a while. Then I decided to take a look for myself.

I found him lying between a bench and the locker-room wall, in a swamp of his own blood, with his street clothes on. A big and ugly giant, and recently dead. Very recently. Judging from the smears on the floor, he'd crawled the last part. He hadn't been going anywhere, though; it was more like an animal looking for a hole to die in.

The way it looked to me, whoever had done it had clubbed him on the head first, with a blunt object about the size of the Eiffel Tower, and then had cut his throat for good measure. Somebody's idea of spade work, maybe. Later on, the medical expert said the skull injury could have been caused in a fall, and maybe so, but it was hard to imagine anybody taking on Odessa Grimes with something as flimsy as a Gillette, and there was no sign of a struggle.

Other than the corpse's with himself.

I bent over him. His jaws hung open at the hinges, but for a weird second I'd have sworn he was trying to whisper something. *Jesus*, maybe. *Sweet Jesus*. But it wasn't Odessa Grimes who was calling on the Good Lord, it was me, and I didn't have to feel his pulse to tell he'd gone up for his last rebound.

Then my mind started stripping gears in a hurry.

My first thought was to get the hell out of there. But it was already too late for that. There was the matter of witnesses, for one: I'd been seen in the gym. Then too, the Law had a shortcut for connecting me with Odessa Grimes. Then, in no particular order, I thought of Roscoe, of Valérie, of a telephone. Somewhere I found a telephone. I tried calling Roscoe: no answer. I tried Valérie: ditto. I got through to my hotel and left a message for her. Then I called the Law. But I was still talking to them when one of their minions, in plain clothes, took the receiver out of my hand and finished the conversation for me.

I mean, the Paris constabulary has been known to move fast on occasion. But not that fast.

Unless, that is, they've been tipped off.

Whoever had gotten Odessa, it turned out, had given them Roscoe. And failing to find Roscoe, they took me.

I spent the rest of that day trying to convince them, first, that they'd made a mistake, and, second, to give me a chance to prove it.

They convinced hard, and looking at it from their point of view, you couldn't blame them. The pressures on the Law are pretty much the same in France as elsewhere, and in the early stages of a case, when the cameras are popping and the bigwigs demanding results, simple arithmetic holds sway. Meaning that, in the eyes of the Police Judiciaire, for every dead body there has to be a live one. Furthermore, I was the only live one they had who wasn't wearing sneakers, and the only one, white or black, who didn't answer them in nigger talk. The basketball players in the P.U.C. gym, it seemed, had gone deaf, dumb, and blind to a man. They'd seen nothing, heard nothing, knew nothing, and they were their own mutual alibi. I was the odd man, and when, in mid-afternoon, they found out that a day or two before I'd been poking around the foreigners' section at the Préfecture, had even "talked" my way into a look at the dossiers on Grimes, Odessa and Hadley, Roscoe, all my hopes of passing myself off as an innocent bystander went up in Gauloise smoke.

By this time we'd moved from the Boulevard St. Michel down to the Quai des Orfèvres. That's a pretty historic corner of Paris—the sightseeing boats go right under your feet and Notre Dame's just a couple of blocks away—but once inside, it's like you never left home. The smell does it mostly, I guess, compounded of dust and nicotine, ink and bad breath, but of fear also and suspicion. A sweaty, metallic smell, inhuman even though it's man-made. The lair of the Law, in sum, and you don't have to have been farther than your friendly L.A.P.D. to know what it's like.

I gave them what I had.

They weren't much impressed with it.

Neither was I. The fact was: I didn't know why Odessa had been killed, unless it was a case of mistaken identity. Nor did I know who had killed him. Nor why, if he was innocent, somebody would have fingered Roscoe Hadley. Nor where Roscoe Hadley was.

And around and around we went. Until I asked to see Dedini.

Dedini wasn't my favorite cop, and no, I probably wouldn't have bought a used car from him. He'd long since risen as far as he was going to in the Police Judiciaire, and he knew it and was bitter about it, and he took out his bitterness on whoever came to hand, including his fellow gendarmes. But he had a kind of brutal realism, born of contempt and experience—some three decades' worth—and I thought I could deal with him.

I had before.

But Odessa Grimes wasn't Dedini's case. Furthermore, Dedini was out on sick leave. Furthermore, it wasn't up to me to decide who I would and wouldn't talk to. Furthermore, if I didn't tell them where they could find Roscoe Hadley, they were going to have me charged with obstructing a police investigation. Etc. Etc. Until, a while later, Monsieur le Commissaire Dedini, Jean-Pierre, stood in the doorway of the office where I'd been being furthermored.

He was a big, ugly man with a square, bulldog head and a pair of rimless glasses that got lost in his jowled face. Despite the mild weather, he wore a sweater under his suit jacket and a raincoat over the lot. You could see why he was on sick leave. He was doing battle with the Paris grippe, but the only weapon he had at hand was a wadded handkerchief, with which he mopped at his forehead and his nose. The handkerchief was visibly getting the worst of it.

"Hello, Monsieur le Commissaire," I said. "I was sorry to hear you were sick. But aren't you rushing the season a little?"

He gazed around the office, at his colleagues, at me. His expression was what I'd once called his scum look. It was habitual, and it took in the whole world.

"What's this shit that you want to talk to me, Monsieur?" he said hoarsely, following the words with a thick cough.

"Alone, Monsieur le Commissaire," I said. "I want to talk to you alone."

I saw the eyebrows go up around the room.

"This isn't my affair," Dedini said with a shrug. "Anything you want to say to me, you can say it now."

"All right," I said, shrugging back at him. "I don't know how much you've been briefed on what's happened. A man called Odessa Grimes has been murdered, a professional basketball player, American, black. I found him. Shortly before I found him, an anonymous caller told the police about it and accused one Roscoe Hadley of having done it. I don't think that's likely. Roscoe Hadley and Odessa Grimes were friends and teammates. These gentlemen here seem to think I know where Hadley can be found. I don't, other than his address, which I've given them. Hadley has troubles of his own, serious ones. It's more likely that the people who murdered Grimes were really after *him*. He may already be dead. If he isn't, the longer you hold me here, the worse our chances of finding him alive."

While I was talking, one of the inspectors who'd been questioning me handed Dedini a sheaf of papers. Among them were the notes he'd been taking. Dedini read through them. He didn't seem to be listening to me. When he'd finished, he looked at me, rheumy-eyed, over the rims of his glasses.

"What do...?" he began. "What do you...?"

But the cough got the better of him. He took out the handkerchief, unwadded it, spat weakly into it, then wadded it back and wiped at his forehead.

"What do you want of me, Monsieur?" he said.

"I want you to tell these gentlemen to let me go. I'm not doing you any good here. I just might be able to on the outside."

I've referred before to a deal I once made with the French Law. Somewhere in the archives of the Police Judiciaire was a copy of the deposition I'd signed. Dedini knew about it. In fact, I'd used his pen. The deposition was a lie which at the time had served the interests of certain people with influence in high places, but it gave me a certain small leverage over the Law. Dedini sighed and sneezed and lumbered out of the office with the Monsieur le Commissaire in charge of the case, Frèrejean by name. I didn't see him again, but when Frèrejean came back some time later, the message he had for me was pure Dedini.

"We'll give you twenty-four hours, Monsieur," he said.

Somehow I doubted it would be enough. On the other hand, when you're dealing with the Law, you learn to take what you can get.

Another thing you learn: you're going to come away feeling dirty. I mean physically, collar-sticking dirty. When I came out on the Quai des Orfèvres, night had already fallen, bringing a damp and germ-laden chill off the Seine, and about all I could think of was a hot bath and a flagon of Glenfiddich, preferably at the same time.

I could have walked to my hotel, but the Giulia was parked out by the curb, between two no-parking signs. It was the first dumb thing she'd done.

I walked around to the driver's side.

"Move over," I said. She did, and I got in. She flung her arms around me and kissed me. I didn't kiss her back.

"Are you all right, Cage?"

"No, I'm not. We'd better find Roscoe. In a hurry."

"I already found him. He's safe, in Neuilly. Just drive, I'll tell you where to go."

I glanced at the rearview as I pulled away from the curb. I stopped for a red light, still on the Île de la Cité, and glanced again.

"Give me the address," I said, when the light switched to green and I turned onto the Boulevard du Palais.

"Why do . . . ?"

"Just do like I say," I said sharply. "Give me the address."

She did.

"Is there a phone?"

There was. She gave me the number.

I headed slowly across the Ile de la Cité toward the Right Bank.

"Now listen carefully. When I get to the Châtelet, I'm going to stop at a newspaper stand. I want you to get out, leaving the door open, then duck around the stand and down into the Métro."

"But I . . ."

"Don't argue. Just do what I tell you."

"I'm sorry, Cage, I didn't . . ."

"Don't look around either. Go down into the Métro. You ought to have enough of a head start. Ride out to Neuilly, but, just in case, don't take the direct line. When you get there, stay there. Keep him there. Above all, don't try to call me. I'll come when I can, but probably not before tomorrow."

The Châtelet Métro station is one of the biggest in Paris. Three lines go through it, meaning they'd have a one-in-six chance of ending up on the same platform she was on if I could reduce them to guessing. "They" was an unmarked Peugeot 304 I'd seen pulling out of a slot behind us on the Quai des Orfèvres. They'd followed us across the Ile de la Cité and the Pont au Change, and when I stopped at the Châtelet kiosk, sure enough they tucked in behind me. I left the motor running when she got out, and it took them a good couple of minutes after she disappeared to realize she wasn't coming back. Then one of them got out to check. I reached across, closed her door, and drove off, followed abruptly by the 304. The last I saw of the one who'd gotten out, he was waving his arms and shouting something after us from the sidewalk, and probably I was too busy congratulating myself to notice that they weren't the only company we had.

I gave the Giulia some exercise just for the hell of it, then drove back to my bathtub. The tail in the 304 was good enough to discourage any ideas I might have had about trying to lose him on the way to Neuilly that same night. In the morning he, or a replacement, was still sitting in the 304 outside the hotel, complete with partner, so I took the Métro myself, losing the partner in a little wrinkle I'd worked out for just such emergencies in the Montparnasse-Bienvenüe station. Then I was in that posh apartment in Neuilly, with Valérie looking out the window again and Roscoe Hadley making a half-assed job at trying to hide the fact that, around the time Odessa Grimes got his throat slit, he, Roscoe, was shacked up in bed with Odessa Grimes' sweetie pie.

4

The 14th Arrondissement of Paris is a mixed bag of a neighborhood that starts at one twentieth-century monument, the Tour Montparnasse, and ends at another, the circular urban autoroute known as the Périphérique. Parts of it are still chic, but behind the Sheraton Hotel extends a so-called "popular" quarter of dingy streets bordered by condemned buildings, boarded-up shop fronts, and narrow, littered sidewalks. Such businesses as survive there are of the low-overhead variety: cheap bars and restaurants, small groceries, dry cleaners, headshops, fly-by-night galleries, and they cater to a populace the only common denominator of which is its lack of political clout, meaning Ayrab, Portuguese, Slav, black, and also the young and transient, and also the old and immobilized.

Marie-Josèphe Lamentin lived in a cul-de-sac off the rue de l'Ouest, a narrow, cobbled alley where you could touch the doors on either side and the rooftops tilted forward, shutting out the sky overhead. The number I wanted could only be reached by walking through another building, then a courtyard where a gang of neighborhood cats was standing guard over some garbage cans. Somebody somewhere was cooking fish. I went up the dark stairs, ducking my head. Marie-Josèphe Lamentin lived on the third floor left, but her doorbell gave off no sound and there was no answer to my knock. I tried the third floor right. I had the impression someone was in, but if so, they didn't want visitors. I retreated then to the ground floor, the courtyard, looked for a concierge, found none, then to the alley, and finally, through a curtain of colored plastic strips, to a storefront bar at the corner.

A group of gents from the wrong side of the Mediterranean were playing cards noisily at a formica-topped table near the front window. The tables behind them were empty except for two of their compatriots who were drinking tea out of glasses in the back and talking to someone, presumably the cook, who stood in a rear doorway. The lighting was harsh, fluorescent, there was the sweaty reek of couscous, and to top off the atmosphere, a jukebox was playing "Heartbreak Hotel," Bedouin version.

The food may have been great, but the service wasn't. I waited at the bar while the card players finished their hand. Then one of them gathered the loose cards and proceeded to shuffle while another, fat and beslippered, with a mustache to compensate for his balding skull, scraped back his chair with a sigh and shambled over to the other side of the counter.

"I'm looking for Mlle. Lamentin," I said to him. "Marie-Josèphe Lamentin. She lives in the passage, number eleven *bis*, third floor left. She's not there now. Do you know where I can find her?"

I had no reason to assume that he should know her. Only he did. Not that he said so, or that there was any change in his bland expression, but when I mentioned her name there was a momentary break in the sound behind me. Even the jukebox seemed to stutter.

"Marie-Josèphe," I repeated. "Do you know her?"

Ayrabs, in my limited experience, are a suspicious race, but if you're not careful, they'll be telling you their life story five minutes after they've met you. All it takes is a little encouragement.

I decided to encourage him.

I ordered a glass of Mescara, that lethal red wine they squeeze in Algeria. I took a hundred-franc note from my wallet and put it on the bar top, making sure he saw there was more where it came from. He wiped his fingers deliberately on his shirt front, then produced a juice glass and a bottle from under the counter. The bottle was about three quarters full and had no label. He filled the glass, put the bottle away, wiped his fingers again. Then he took the hundred-franc note, looked at it, turned it over on the other side, looked at it, and, presumably satisfied, made change.

I left the change where it was.

"Marie-Josèphe Lamentin. She has, or had, a boy friend called Grimes. Odessa Grimes. A black American. The black man who's been murdered."

The barman shrugged.

"Do you know her?" I said.

"I don't know her," he answered.

"Or him?"

There was a mirror behind the bar, and I could see the card players watching me through it while pretending not to.

"Look," I said, "I'm not the police. I'm not even French. I just want to talk to her. I was a friend of Odessa Grimes, the black man."

I said it loud enough for the whole bar to hear, but nobody answered, and when I turned toward them, the card players looked the other way.

Your friendly neighborhood saloon, in sum.

I sipped at the wine. It had a taste that would have taken some acquiring. The card game stopped and the conversation died off. The only noise was that lovesick singsong from the jukebox, and the bartender stared at me with the patient, unseeing stare his people had learned when the French invaded the Casbah. Odessa Grimes had been murdered; his sweetie pie had known about it. Roscoe Hadley had been shacked up with her at the time, and the first inkling he'd had of what had happened was when he'd started worrying about Odessa coming back and finding them between the sheets.

Because Marie-Josèphe Lamentin had told him not to worry, that Odessa wouldn't be coming back.

Which had driven Roscoe Hadley out of his skull, or at least out into the streets.

According to Roscoe Hadley.

A fly crawled across my change.

I sipped some more wine, and the fly flew off. The bartender's eyes flicked away from mine, then blandly returned, and there was a sudden burst of conversation from the table behind me.

Not much of a signal, but enough of a one.

I went out through the plastic curtain in a hurry, leaving the Allah-worshipers to fight over my change.

"Mlle. Lamentin!" I yelled after her. "Marie-Josèphe!"

It's funny how often oversized studs team up with little bits of women. By Parisian standards Marie-Josèphe Lamentin wasn't that small, but even in the three-inch heels she wore, she couldn't have come up to Odessa's Adam's apple. In respects other than the center jump, though, she looked like she could more than hold her own. Her calves were thin but muscular, her tight-skirted ass had an independent strut. Her make-up was heavy and gray on the lips, and her lower lip protruded in that perpetual thick pout characteristic of the girls from down Pointe-à-Pitre way.

Maybe she heard me call her, but she didn't stop. I caught up with her in the inner courtyard.

"Marie-Josèphe," I repeated, taking her arm.

She half-turned, not seeing, then yanked her arm free and headed into the second entryway.

"It's too early," she said in an annoyed hiss. "Go away. I'm busy."

"I only want to talk to you. I'm a friend of Roscoe's. Of Odessa's too."

"Idiot!" she said, shaking free again. "I'm busy, can't you see?"

She started up the stairs. I followed, to the independent beguine of her behind.

I caught up with the rest of her at her landing. She fumbled in her bag for her key, then opened the door and went inside.

I followed.

The apartment was one room with a slanting, dirt-smudged skylight. Some plants hung from pots mounted on the walls, but otherwise the furnishings were nondescript. The bed was the principal object. It was covered with a large, multi-colored, India-cotton spread.

"All right, then," said Marie-Josèphe, turning to me. "But it will cost you double."

"How much is double?"

"Two hundred francs."

"I only want to talk to you."

"Talk or make love, it's all the same. Two hundred francs."

I gave her the money. She kicked off her shoes and wriggled out of her skirt. She had nothing on under the skirt. She curled her body on the bedspread, her legs tucked under her, her blouse still on, and shook loose her black, curly hair and stared out in front of her, not at me, in a pose that was smoky, sullen, full-lipped. Her skin was the color of café au lait.

"You go in for plants," I said.

"What?"

"I said: You seem to go in for plants."

"Is that what you want to talk about?"

"No. It's just something I wouldn't have expected of Odessa's girl friend." She didn't react. "You are Odessa Grimes' girl friend, aren't you?"

"I knew him."

"You know what happened to him, then?"

"Yes." Matter-of-factly.

"You don't seem particularly grieved about it."

She didn't disagree, or agree either. She just shrugged a little.

"He did this to me," she said. With an index finger, she pulled the skin taut under one eye, and bending over her, I could see what the heavy make-up largely hid: red welts on the cheekbone and, above, the remnants of a black eye.

"Did he beat you up a lot?"

"When he felt like it."

"When did he feel like it?"

She shrugged again, a dull, uncaring gesture.

"When you messed around with other men? Like Roscoe Hadley?"

The name brought a trace of smile to the corners of her mouth.

"He's sweet, Roscoe."

"Is that why Odessa beat you up? Because you were messing around with Roscoe?"

"I wasn't messing around with Roscoe."

"That's not what he says. What about yesterday, for instance?" She didn't answer, though more from lassitude, you'd have said, than from having anything to hide. "Wasn't Roscoe here yesterday? From, say, the late morning till the middle of the afternoon?"

"Yesterday?"

"Yesterday," I said.

"I didn't see Roscoe all day yesterday." Tonelessly.

"Listen, Marie-Josèphe. This is important. Roscoe says he came here yesterday morning to pick Odessa up. Only Odessa had already left. And one thing led to another and he ended up balling you till the middle of the afternoon. Isn't that the truth?"

"I didn't see Roscoe all day yesterday."

It wasn't just what she said but the way she said it: that vague and smoky-voiced refrain. I reached for her arm, as though by accident, but she shifted toward the center of the bed.

As though by accident.

"Don't you realize that by saying that you're getting Roscoe into a hell of a lot of trouble? You knew Odessa was going to get it, didn't you? Did you also know they were going to finger Roscoe for it? But Roscoe wasn't there, Marie-Josèphe. He didn't kill anybody. He was here, with you. You're his alibi. But lest you forget, he's yours too."

This didn't seem to fluster her, not in the slightest. She shrugged again.

"Didn't you tell me you weren't a cop?" she said.

"I didn't tell you anything. My name's Cage. Here's my card."

I took one out of my wallet and reached it toward her. But I went past the card and grabbed for her arm. She tried to yank away. Then, caught, she became a bundle of twisting muscle. She thrashed like a trapped cat and cursed and carved wildly at my face with her free hand.

I caught the free hand and pinned her against me. She was on her knees on the bed, held fast, and her hair spun and flailed at my eyes, her teeth flashed, and her body contracted into a single muscle, sprung, contracted, sprung. I held on, forcing her head back with my own. She had a cheap, animal smell, and I could feel her body beating like a pulse, and the beat came inside me and did a high-assed beguine down into my scrotum.

She felt me go hard. It made her giggle, softly.

"I'll suck you if you like," I heard her say softly. "Anything you like."

I held on. After a while I felt her subside, go dead, limp. Then I pulled one sleeve of her blouse up past the elbow, found what I was looking for, then released her and stood clear.

"Is that why Odessa beat you up?" I said.

She stayed on her knees, rocking a little. Her arms were folded, and her hands rubbed at the inner elbows. Rubbed hard, like they could make the needle marks go away. And the smoke went in and out of her eyes and nobody had lit a match.

I repeated the question.

She seemed to hear it this time. It made her laugh, a high-pitched mulatto laugh, the kind that's got sass and chagrin mixed up in it. It didn't last long.

"Odessa beat me up?" she said. "That man beat me up when I *didn't!*"

"You mean he was supplying you with dope?"

"Supplying? Yeah. That man was supplying me with everything. Everything I needed, everything I didn't."

"And now that he's gone?"

"Gone?"

"Dead, Marie-Josèphe. Odessa's dead, remember? Murdered."

"Yeah. Don't need that man. Never did need him."

"Who killed him, Marie-Josèphe? Why was he killed? Who got you to keep Roscoe here yesterday while Odessa got his?"

"He's sweet, Roscoe," she crooned, gray-lipped.

"You sure freaked the hell out of him, Marie-Josèphe. When he lit out of here yesterday, it was a wonder he didn't get run over in the street. Or was that the idea?"

She looked up at me. Suddenly the smoke was gone from her eyes. It didn't become her.

"I told him to run, M'sieu," she said. "I can't help him. I told him to run away."

"Don't be a fool, Marie-Josèphe. Sooner or later the police are going to ask you the same questions. They won't be as nice as I am, and they won't pay for the answers. Probably they'll break all your needles while they're at it."

For an instant she looked scared, but only an instant. Then her eyes went small, tired, professional.

"Time's up, M'sieu," she said, uncoiling from the bed. She picked up her skirt from the floor.

"Maybe I'd like to go again," I said.

She shook her head.

"You've had your money's worth," she said, putting on her skirt and stepping up into her shoes. "Some other time."

"Don't be a fool," I repeated. "Nobody's going to protect you for very long."

"Maybe you're the one who's being the fool, M'sieu," she said, looking past me at the door. And in a way, she was right.

=5=

The trouble with your average French thug is that he's seen the same movie too many times. Maybe Belmondo could get away with imitating Bogart in *Le Deuxième Souffle,* but the French thug imitating Belmondo imitating Bogart is one too many, like a story that loses something in the retelling. For instance, the one who was holding the gun had a cigarette stuck in his mouth, but the cigarette was unlit, and when the time came for us to go and him to crush it under his heel, on Marie-Josèphe's floor... well, it was just a waste of a cigarette.

The one without a gun worried me more. They usually do. He was a quiet wimp of a guy with an odd way of bobbing and weaving his head, and I put him down for a knife-and-scissors specialist. The Belmondo did most of the talking, but it was the little guy who shook me down, and when we left Marie-Josèphe's—going for a conversation, they said—the little guy led the way, with me in the middle and the Belmondo making with the cannon behind me.

Marie-Josèphe may have had every reason to be scared, but she didn't show it. She looked past me like I was just another trick, and her last words were for them.

"I didn't tell him a thing," she said.

They had a black 504 parked at the rue de l'Ouest end of the alley. A driver sat behind the wheel, reading *France Soir.* The Belmondo got in front with him, the wimp in back with me. Sure enough, when I looked across, the wimp had a shiv out in his palm. The blade was open, and it ran past the end of his fingertips. He grinned when he saw that I'd noticed it. Meanwhile the Belmondo had stuck another cigarette in his mouth. This one he lit. It was the brown-paper kind—Bastos or Celtique—and it stunk like cheap grass.

I made a try or two at the conversation we were supposed to have, but nobody was in a talking mood. We drove out of the warren of streets onto the avenue du Maine, then up through the traffic to the Alésia church, then across to René-Coty and up toward the Parc Montsouris. The park is one of those keep-off-the-grass Paris showplaces, with enormous spreading trees and swans floating on the lake and a small nineteenth-century observatory up on the hill, and all that mars it is that the old Sceaux line, now a branch of the Métro, runs through an open gully up the middle of it. We drove into the sun along the west edge of the park, then abruptly onto a cobbled street that curved up between rows of handsome, ivy-covered private homes. They would have belonged in a well-heeled suburb. But this wasn't a suburb, it was Paris, meaning you had to be better than well-heeled to live there. Enough better, say, to keep a couple of stiffs outside your front door in another 504, just in case you needed the parking space.

To judge, Didier "Dédé" Delatour was doing just fine. I'd never had the pleasure, but I knew the name. Dédé Delatour was Mafioso modern-style, meaning the kind it's considered chic to have at your dinner table or in your neighborhood discothèque. His above-board wealth came from being a "sportsman," meaning he owned a racing stable as well as a piece of several go-go gambling joints on the Côte d'Azur. What went on below the surface nobody knew for sure, but he'd been connected to enough shady operations to give Parisian thrill-seekers just the right kind of shiver. What's more, he was good-looking in a dark, Mediterranean sort of way, with the Mediterranean accent to go with it, and, to top off the image, back in the past he'd done time. Not a lot, but time.

This made him the genuine article.

I was ushered upstairs into a hexagonal salon with a view down onto a garden that had a well-tended lawn, tall stone planters, and assorted statuary on pedestals. My escort was dismissed, and Dédé Delatour himself came on, self-assured and affable and flashing of tooth, in a dark flannel suit that was cut just a little tight, as though to remind you of the macho and muscle which had put him where he was. He gave me the glad hand and a sentence or two of pretty approximate English. He offered me a seat, a drink, and a cigar. I refused the last two, sank into a soft divan, and lit my pipe, puzzled by his bonhommie, while he apologized for any rough treatment I might have had. He wanted to know how things were in California. I said I hadn't been there for a while. He said he'd always wanted to go to California—" 'ollyvood," the girls, the sunshine, the skyscrapers, the big cars. And sports, the betting, fabulous. In France they had no sports betting, only horses. A little boxing. But it would come. It had in Spain, Italy, England. A question of organization. But he'd never had the time for California. It was business, always business, I knew how that was, didn't I?

At this point Dédé Delatour unleashed his eyebrows. He had thick, mobile ones, and a bristling mustache to go with them, and he did a lot of work with both.

I'd surprised him, he said. I had what I wanted, didn't I? Wasn't Adlay what I wanted? It was too bad, such an excellent athlete, the public liked him, he scored many points. He would be hard to replace. But business was business, he was willing to let me have Adlay. *Alors...?*

Alors is French for *then*. The way he used it called for me to take up the conversational ball. At least to tell him he'd made a mistake about me.

I didn't.

In addition there was the matter of Greemse.

"What is your interest in Greemse, Monsieur? Why have you been bothering about him and his whore? He wasn't even part of our arrangement. On the contrary..."

He left it hanging there, his eyebrows up, and I realized he'd jumped to a conclusion about me. It may have been a cockeyed one, but at least it explained the kid-glove reception, and if it was cockeyed, even simple-minded, you have to remember that he was French. Because just like if you told the average Frenchman you came from Chicago he'd assume you were a cousin of Al Capone, so to Dédé Delatour an American from California who'd been hanging around Roscoe Hadley was no garden-variety basketball freak. And the fact that this particular Californian lived in Paris and spoke passable French only proved that he was fronting for others who didn't.

Or so it seemed to me, on the spot. The fact that there could be another, more plausible explanation didn't so much as occur to me.

"Maybe that's just the point," I said, taking the bait. "That Grimes wasn't part of the arrangement."

"*Comment?*" he said. Then: "Ahhh..." and the eyebrows relaxed. It was as though I'd just explained a lot of things. "But don't forget, Monsieur, we don't *own* the basketball clubs ourselves. Not all of them, not yet. Greemse's and Adlay's club only just came up from the lower division this season. The club owner signed them to play without consulting us. But now, with them gone, it will be much simpler."

"How is that?"

"Obviously. Without them, their club is no longer competitive. Where will they find two other players of such quality? They will have to be replaced... by you, of course. But only after the club has been put up for sale. Cheaply."

"Obviously," I said. "But did Grimes have to be murdered for that to happen?"

Dédé Delatour shrugged, with his eyebrows as well as his shoulders.

"Maybe you should ask Adlay about it."

"Maybe I did."

"What did he say?"

"Maybe he says he doesn't know why Grimes was killed."

"Gr... How do you say it in American?" He made another stab at "Grimes," but it just wouldn't come. "Greemse," he said, chuckling. "There's no reason for us to mourn him. He was a troublemaker. The Italians didn't want him, the Spanish either. A nigger hoodlum of low intelligence. Not even the other players liked him."

"You mean he got his throat cut just because he didn't get along with the other players?"

Again the double shrug.

"Perhaps he had begun to meddle where he wasn't wanted."

"Meddle in what?"

Dédé Delatour looked at me strangely. He didn't answer. I decided to take a shot at it.

"Like in the dope trade?" I persisted.

It lay there between us. We stared at each other, and suddenly it was like each of us had things to hide. Then his eyebrows made a frowning *v* over his nose, and he repeated:

"Where he wasn't wanted."

That too lay there a moment.

"Please remember, Monsieur," Dédé Delatour said evenly, "our relationship is based strictly on *le basket*. You supply the players, we arrange for contracts and payments. It is a small business now. It could be a much bigger one."

"Could be?"

"*Will* be." The flash came back into his eyes. "We are creating something from the bottom," he said, gesturing. "The European project is getting people excited. The right people. We will have our European league. It will take time, that's all. We must all be patient. But once this little... episode... is out of the way, our control can only emerge reinforced."

"Yes," I said. "But meanwhile there's a problem."

"What problem?"

"Hadley."

"That's what I don't understand."

"Somebody has been setting him up for Grimes' murder."

"Setting up...? Ah, yes, the police. I heard you spent yesterday afternoon with them yourself." The idea seemed to amuse him. "You were the one who discovered the body, weren't you?"

"That's right."

"An unfortunate coincidence."

"Maybe so, maybe not. But was it a coincidence that somebody tipped the police off to Hadley?"

"Did they? Perhaps that was just a little joke." He chuckled at it. "Our police have no sense of humor."

"Neither did Grimes when he was slit ear to ear."

"I don't see..."

"Simply that Grimes was murdered with a knife, and one of your boys seems pretty handy with the cutlery."

"You mean Jeannot?"

"I don't know his name. The little guy. And here's another coincidence that may or may not be one. The woman Hadley was with at the time. Now she claims she never saw him yesterday."

"What woman is that?"

"Come on, Monsieur Delatour. Her name is Marie-Josèphe Lamentin."

"Ah, you mean Greemse's whore?" He dismissed her with a waving gesture. "That one will say whatever she is told to say, Monsieur."

The message, then, was clear enough. Whatever the real reasons for Odessa Grimes' murder, it had been used as a warning. Against me, presumably, and the people I presumably worked for. For a minute there I thought I had Roscoe all but off the hook.

All but.

"Now, Monsieur," said Dédé Delatour, "I've answered your questions. I'll tell Jeannot you made the connection, it will flatter him. And rest assured, the whore can be taken care of, and also, if need be, the police. But I, in turn, have something to ask you."

"Go ahead," I said.

"Why haven't you disposed of Adlay?"

It was the $64,000 Special, the one we've all been waiting for, and, logical as it may have been from Delatour's point of view, I had no ready answer.

"Hadley is our business," I said finally, keeping my voice level.

"Yes, of course," with a magnanimous wave. "Just as Greemse was ours. But who is *our*, Monsieur? Who is *us*?"

There was suddenly nothing for me to say or do. It was his hand, and his to play.

"I mean, I've heard what Adlay did to you people. Revenge lasts a long time, and in our business there's only one way that revenge is exacted, isn't that so? Yet you've kept him alive, and that I don't understand. Unless, that is..."—with a knowing smile—"... Adlay's concubine has had something to do with it?"

Marie-Josèphe, I noticed, was Grimes' whore, whereas Valérie got off as Hadley's concubine, but I had no time to dwell on the semantic implications.

"A resourceful bitch," said Dédé Delatour with a certain savor. "Right down to her hideaway. Who would ever think of looking in Neuilly for an American nigger who measures two meters?"

"You're pretty well informed," I said.

"It's my business," he answered. And so it was, and I was duly impressed. But then he had to go and lay it on, in true macho style. He gave me a run-down on the last few days, not only of Roscoe Hadley's movements and his concubine's, but also of mine. Which touched my professional nerve. I mean, I like to think I can spot company with my eyes shut and plugs in my ears.

"Then what now?" said Dédé Delatour.

"That's our business," I repeated.

"So I'd have thought. But it occurs to me now that maybe you need help with Adlay. It wouldn't be difficult. Unless, that is— much as I'd hate to think it—that he was trying to make a separate deal with you?"

I shook my head.

"*Alors...?*"

There it was again, inviting an answer.

The ploy I tried may have been a dumb one, but it was the only one in sight.

"It may be," I said, staring at him, "that we don't want to dispose of him. It may be that we have other uses for him."

He didn't take to that, not at all. The eyebrows went up thickly, and at the same time his brow tensed.

"What uses?"

"Suppose," I said reflectively. "Just suppose all we want is for him to go on playing basketball?"

It was a dumb ploy, as I say, in that it was dangerous, and dangerous because I could only see half the implications. But the half I could see had distinct possibilities. Like what it might mean, when the small business of *le basket* became big and the betting began and the fix went in, to have an experienced fixer like Roscoe Hadley already seeded into the game, at star level, with the right kind of control on him. I was pretty well convinced that Dédé Delatour could be made to see it too, and not only Dédé Delatour but, if necessary, the California Connection that supplied him with basketball bodies. And even—given his precarious circumstances—Roscoe Hadley.

But then the telephone had to go and wreck it.

It was an intercom system, giving off an intermittent buzz instead of a ring, and the apparatus was on a small desk in a corner of the room by the window. I could only see Delatour's face in profile when he answered, but it was clear from his tone that somebody had fucked up. Badly. Whoever was at the other end of the line apparently wasn't the one who'd fucked up, but he had to take it as if he was. And Dédé Delatour knew how to dish it out all right. When he was done, he listened a moment, his mouth tight, then barked an order and banged down the receiver. Or started to. Then he pulled it back, jabbed a call button, ordered, "Come up here *now!*"

Then he laid the receiver down. Gently. Then gently took a cigar from a humidor while he gazed down on the garden, and ran the cigar back and forth under his nose, and put it down.

Gently.

When he turned back to me there was a crooked smile on his

face, not the one he wore at dinner tables. I realized it was his way of telling me the fuzz was off the peach.

The message registered, but too late. By then the door to the room had opened and the Belmondo came in. He closed the door behind him and stood next to it. He had his cannon out, and at a nod from his boss, he pointed it at me.

"I don't get it," I said. "In fact, if you ask me, this is a hell of a way to treat a partner."

"You've been telling us fairy tales," snapped Dédé Delatour.

"Fairy tales?" I said. "I don't have the foggiest idea what you're talking about."

The eyebrows again, up, but not for long. The smile again, the crooked one. It cracked the skin on his cheeks.

"I don't understand what your game is. Yet. But do you really want me to believe you don't know what's happened?"

"Believe what you want," I said, feeling his tension.

"Your friends. The nigger and the blonde bitch. While we've been talking. They've gone, disappeared. We've lost them."

Dédé Delatour was quick on his feet, quicker with his hands, and I didn't have time to duck. He came at me with two slaps, forehand and backhand, short, sharp, and stinging.

I caught them flush in the face. I saw stars all right, white on a black field, then black on a white, and the next thing I saw, when I started forward, was the Belmondo coming in from the side, gun barrel high.

Also the last thing, for a while.

Give me a V for Valor if you must, but the Belmondo was quick too, and he hit harder than he was supposed to in the script.

6

I never did like being flim-flammed by well-heeled blondes. Neither, I guess, did Dédé Delatour. The thing was: I had nothing by way of compensation. Whereas Dédé Delatour had me.

I had plenty of time to think about the injustice of this, that long night in his dungeon. At least during the early parts of it. After a while, I didn't think about much of anything.

A word about the well-heeled blonde, though. She was born Merchadier, and if the name means nothing to you, to the average Parisian it's as familiar as his morning croissant. Valérie's father was just the latest in a long line of Maître Merchadiers who have pleaded before the French bar, with consistent success and celebrity and, in the case of Valérie's father, a penchant for unpopular causes. Valérie's mother was a Yankee beauty who'd surfaced in Paris after the war and stayed long enough to find a husband, bear a child, and win a handsome alimony settlement which, in the time-honored way of Yankee beauties, she'd subsequently cashed in for a title. Valérie grew up, thusly, on the estate of a Scottish laird. She was back in Paris, though, in time for the barricades of May '68, took simultaneous degrees in Law and Political Science, then was shipped off to Harvard Law School, which she quit after a year to run off with a youth variously described as a radical anarchist, a communard, and a garage mechanic. This exotic venture foundered somewhere south of Katmandu, where there were no garages and the money ran out and the (respective) families had to be prevailed upon for plane tickets to their (respective) homes. Ever since, Valérie had kicked around the world, though mostly around Paris, where she was as at home with the chic discothèque crowd at Chez Castel as in the joints north of Les Halles, where the coffee has mud at the bottom and the *kif,* as it's called, is flown in daily from Casablanca. Kicking around, in addition, with a series of unpopular causes of her own, who had as common denominator a certain talent between the sheets.

A daughter of the century, in sum. If you want to add that she had a living-up-to-papa hang-up, well, that's your privilege. As it would be to say that among her "unpopular causes" would have to be listed black basketball players from the streets of Los Angeles.

My last words to her had been to keep Roscoe in the Neuilly apartment till she heard from me. Her last words to Delatour's Neuilly stake-out had apparently been *"Haut les mains,"* which means "Reach for the sky" in local jargon. How she'd spotted him, or coaxed him up to the apartment, I could only guess. Like Delatour had said, she was a resourceful bitch. But by the time they were finished with him, Roscoe had apparently slam-dunked him into the bathtub and they'd taken all his toys. Including his car keys.

So much for last words.

Dédé Delatour's dungeon wasn't really much of a dungeon. It was a downstairs room with a window fronting on the garden. There weren't any bars on the window, and all that separated the garden from the street beyond it was a spiked wrought-iron fence. It would have been easy for me, when I came to, to go out the window, jump the fence, and head off into the beautiful Paris night. The only trouble was that when I came to, my hands were tied behind a chair and my ankles to the chair legs and Dédé Delatour's muscle were taking turns beating out the *"Marseillaise"* on the only body I had.

I won't go into the more sordid details. It's not the first time it's happened to me. Hoods the world over seem to take naturally to beating up on people—it's good, I guess, for their muscle tone—and there's not much difference in techniques. Suffice it to say that they hurt, particularly Jeannot, the little wimp, and that it was a long, long night. But there wasn't much for me to do but say "Ouch" and tell them whatever fairy tales I could think of and pass out when they got carried away in their enthusiasm.

The best of my fairy tales was that we'd all been caught up in a big misunderstanding, that whatever they wanted to do with Roscoe Hadley was fine with me, only that they should count me out, I had a lost-and-found service for overfed Americans to worry about and no special interest in basketball or the dope traffic or Odessa Grimes' murder or whatever it was that had got their boss so exercised. But the truth has a way of paling under such circumstances, meaning that they didn't go for that one overly. Whereas the one they wanted to hear—about where Hadley and the girl were—I didn't know. This pissed them off, and whenever the little wimp got really pissed off, he'd pull my chair back by pulling my hair and belt me in the mouth, or now and then in the Adam's apple.

A long night, like I say.

It ended. Even the longest ones do.

Put it that Dédé Delatour didn't like eating his breakfast alone.

When they took me back upstairs, I remember, he was drinking coffee in a raw-silk dressing gown. The dressing gown was wine-colored. There was a tray on a coffee table and two silver pots on the tray, one for coffee, one for milk, and a plate with some crumbs on it. Dédé Delatour, looking fresh like a flower, was lighting up his first cigar of the morning. He was his old affable self again. Whereas for me, I hurt so much, all over, that it was a kind of relief not to feel a thing below my wrists and ankles.

"Did you have a good night?" he asked when I'd been dumped on the divan across from him.

"I've had worse," I managed. My voice wobbled at a high pitch, like it had been changed back. My upper lip was novocaine-stiff.

"How about some coffee?"

It seemed like a promising idea. I nodded. Somebody poured me a cup and I leaned over to take it. I couldn't handle the cup, though. It bobbled in my hand, and I spilled the lot on his mahogany. Nobody gave me a refill.

"Now," said Delatour, dispensing with the niceties, "what is your interest in Adlay?"

"I don't have any interest," I said.

Apparently this was the wrong answer. Delatour motioned with his cigar and somebody slapped me on the side of the head. For some reason, the slap helped straighten out my larynx. It hurt, my larynx, but I found I could use it.

"I wanted to keep him from getting killed," I said.

"By whom?"

"People in California. Your partners."

"Why did they want to kill him?"

"You know why."

"I want to hear it from you."

I remember it hurting me to talk, and figuring that he knew it hurt. But whenever I muffed my lines, the cigar waved and there was the slap on the head. A double bind, I think they call it in psychology. In any case, the dialogue, minus slaps, went something like this:

CAGE: He was once involved in an ugly business. Back in California.
DELATOUR: What kind of ugly business?
CAGE: Fixing games. He was a college basketball star. He and some other players were accused of fixing games.
DELATOUR: Do you mean they lost intentionally?
CAGE: No. It worked on points.
DELATOUR: Points?
CAGE: You bet a team to win by ten points. It wins by eight. You lose.
DELATOUR: An interesting idea. A team doesn't have to lose, it just wins by less?
CAGE: That's right.
DELATOUR: And that's illegal in America?
CAGE: If you do it on purpose.
DELATOUR: And Adlay did this?
CAGE: They were accused of it. There was what's called a grand-jury investigation. It made a lot of headlines. The other players all testified that they were innocent. It got them banned from basketball, but it kept them out of jail.
DELATOUR: What about Adlay?
CAGE: He was the one everybody was waiting for. The big fish. He was supposed to be the star witness.
DELATOUR: What happened? Did he confess?
CAGE: No. He didn't show. He disappeared.
DELATOUR: Disappeared? Why was that such a bad thing?
CAGE: It meant he was guilty by implication. Also it gave the grand jury, and the public, the impression that certain people had helped him disappear. Such as your partners. This was very embarrassing to them.
DELATOUR: I can see that. But what happened to him then?
CAGE: He stayed disappeared. He left the country, changed his name, stayed away from basketball. Until now.
DELATOUR: Until now?
CAGE: Until now.
DELATOUR: How long ago was it that this happened?
CAGE: Four, five years.
DELATOUR: But they—these people in California—still want him disposed

of? After all this time?

CAGE: You said it yourself: 'Revenge lasts a long time.'

This seemingly innocent quotation brought the cigar into motion again. It was Jeannot, the little wimp, who started for me. He was a tireless bastard. I can see him still, the flat head, the quick eyes in a small, impassive face, as he moved in to do what he did best. It freaked me out. I tried to ward him off and at the same time I hollered. And not only hollered but blubbered, stammered, yammered, and all the other things grown men aren't supposed to do in public. And I shouted at Dédé Delatour:

"If you don't believe me, call them! For Christ's sake, call them and ask! All you've got to do is pick up the fucking phone!"

Delatour smiled at me—not the crooked one but the dinner-table special.

He called off the wimp.

"I already have, Monsieur," he said. "Last night. I didn't want to—one never likes to disturb one's associates with trivial questions—but you obliged me to. With your fairy tales."

"All right!" I blurted out. "And what did they say?"

He shook his head from side to side, then leaned forward and stubbed out his cigar.

"It's all the same to them," he said, straightening up. "Adlay— or whatever his name is—is old business." The smile came back, bigger and flashing of teeth. "They don't give a royal fuck what happens to him. As long as it happens in Europe."

The news hit me like a ton. It was like somebody had just told me: Hey fella, the world's not round, it's a cube and right over here's where you fall off. I'd been flim-flammed all right, and beaten to an omelette for my pains, but right then I couldn't think by whom. Oh sure, by a blonde, but also by a spade called Roscoe, and maybe

Odessa too, defunct, and in addition by everybody who came into my head, from the Bobby Goldsteins, father and son, to old Mrs. Hotchkiss in the Third Grade. By everybody and nobody in sum, and they were all there in my head, having a fine old rampage, and I couldn't put any of it together then, there was too much noise from the party inside.

Dédé Delatour was trying to tell me something. It had to do with his partners in California, Johnny Vee and friends. Something to the effect that I wasn't part of their organization, that they hadn't hired me after all. Oh, but they knew me all right, our paths had crossed before. And Delatour was asking me some question, asked it more than once. But the numbness was leaving my lips now, and they felt big like rubber tires, and somewhere between them and my brain there must have been an accident because the traffic was piled up for miles in both directions.

"I asked them what they wanted me to do with you," Delatour was saying. His eyebrows were up. It looked like they were held there by sky-hooks. "*Alors*...? Don't you want to know what they said?"

By way of answer, he had his arm out, fist extended. Then he inverted his fist in the classic gesture: thumb down.

Hail Fucking Caesar.

He seemed to find this a real rib-tickler. He threw his head back and roared.

Around in there, somehow or other, the choreography changed. Don't ask me how, but one minute the table was between us and the next it wasn't and we were both on our feet and Dédé Delatour was glad-handing me like we'd just met.

It was crazy, kind of. We were both about the same height, but I had the impression I was standing on my ankles.

"Don't worry about it, *mon vieux*," he was telling me. "I like you too much for that. I think I'm really starting to like you. Besides, California is . . . what? Nine hours, ten thousand kilometers away? A long way off. We can take care of our own affairs, can't we. Besides, if they don't want Adlay, I do. Isn't that right? I think I want him more than you do, more even than the police. Isn't that right?"

"That's right," I said.

It was crazy, like I said.

"*Alors, mon vieux*. We're going to find him, aren't we? You and I? I'll be looking for him too, of course, but I've the feeling you'll be the one who's going to find him, yes I do. And that you'll bring him to me. Yes?"

He actually put his arm around my shoulder. Then he motioned to the Belmondo, who was holding up the wall next to the door. The Belmondo stuck his cannon inside his belt and stood aside, and Dédé Delatour walked me to the door in his dressing gown, with his arm around my shoulder.

"Then it'll be time for us to have another talk," he said, patting me. "I'll be looking forward to it, *mon vieux*. About Adlay's future, yes? But about yours too."

I don't know how I got out of there, less about how I got home. Only that I did.

The desk clerk at the hotel had some messages for me, plus an unpleasant piece of news for which he kept trying to apologize. He also wanted to know if I wanted him to call a doctor.

I told him to forget about the apology. Also about the doctor.

All I wanted to do was go to bed.

This I did.

=7=

They were there when I woke up. The one called Frèrejean was mucking around at my dresser. The other was just coming out of the bathroom in his shirt sleeves. He had one sleeve rolled up, like he'd been checking the drains. Neither one of them so much as blushed when they saw me looking at them.

I was lying on top of the bed with all my clothes on. I'd been dreaming. It was one of those dreams where you make up a story to make the pain go away, and it does, but then when the story's over, the pain comes back, so you have to make up another story. Only this time Monsieur le Commissaire Frèrejean was standing by my dresser and the plumber was just coming out of the bathroom, and the pain was back and throbbing, and there was no other story.

They were in no rush. The plumber put on his suit jacket and they went into the sitting room and waited while somehow or other I got myself into the bathroom. I surveyed the victim rockily. All in all, you could say that Delatour's muscle had done a pretty professional job. My left eye was mostly closed, and the skin around it had already started to turn blue. Otherwise there wasn't much visible, and when I pried my lips apart, my teeth were standing in ranks, all present and accounted for. No broken bones either, only forget-me-nots of hurt whenever I breathed or swallowed. I took a hot shower, then a cold one, and did what I could to repair the damage.

Then I dressed, slowly, and by the time I got out into the sitting room I was feeling some approximation of human.

Also hungry-human.

It was the middle of the afternoon. Mentally I tipped the desk clerk for having held them off that long.

"Is it going to take a while?" I asked them.

That would depend on me.

"Well, long or short, I'm going to eat something. Do you want anything?"

They would accept coffee, yes, but nothing else, thank you. I ordered up coffee for three and sandwiches for one, plus various other things that came into my mind while I pictured the sandwiches. But when the waiter brought it all up, about all I could get past my swollen gullet was the Glenfiddich.

"Well," I asked them, "did you find anything interesting, looking around? Or were you just browsing?"

"Where is Adlay, Monsieur?" Frèrejean countered blandly. "Where is Valérie Merchadier?"

Them too. It was getting to be a refrain.

"I take it you'd have found them if they were here."

"That's not what I asked you, Monsieur."

"I know it's not what you asked me. I also know you gave me twenty-four hours to produce him. Well? I failed."

"You led us a merry chase, Monsieur," said Frèrejean imperturbably. "Now it's over. You will please answer my question."

"I don't know where they are."

"You did yesterday, didn't you?"

"That's right. Until early afternoon."

"Where were they?"

I gave him the Neuilly address. Not that it would do him much good now.

He jotted it down in a pocket-sized notebook.

"Then what happened?"

"Then I went off to try to prove Hadley hadn't killed Odessa Grimes. I ran into a little trouble. I'd told them to stay in the apartment. They didn't. I haven't seen them since."

"You realize, I presume, that at the least you can be charged with obstructing a police investigation?"

This pissed the hell out of me. There I was staring at them out of one eye, and like it would have been clear to anybody but a blind Mongoloid that I hadn't been obstructing anything lately except with my face. But they either couldn't see it or wouldn't.

"Go ahead," I said. "Charge me."

Up to this point Frèrejean had done the talking, but the next question came from the plumber.

"Did you?" he asked.

"Did I what?"

"Did you prove he didn't kill Odessa Grimes?"

"Yes. At least to my own satisfaction."

"How?" This from Frèrejean again.

"When Grimes was killed, Hadley was otherwise occupied."

"What does that mean?"

"It means that he was fucking a woman."

"Valèrie Merchadier?"

"No. Her name is Lamentin. She was Grimes' girl friend, at least some of the time. Marie-Josèphe Lamentin. You may have some trouble getting her to admit it. About Hadley, I mean. I did. But, then, your methods are better than mine."

I spelled the name, started to give the address. But Frèrejean wasn't writing.

"We already talked to her," he said. "She corroborates what you've said. She's given Adlay his alibi."

An interesting, if surprising, piece of information. Assuming, as I did, that Dédé Delatour had set Roscoe up, then something had happened in the last twenty-four hours to change his mind.

"When did you talk to her?" I asked.

"That's no concern of yours," Frèrejean replied. "The question remains: if Adlay can prove his innocence, why has he run away?"

"I don't know. Roscoe's a big boy. Maybe he's afraid you won't give him the chance. He can read the papers too. Or maybe there are other people who want him as much as you do."

"What people?" asked the plumber.

"What people what?"

"Want Hadley?"

"Dédé Delatour, for instance," I said, with a casual shrug. If I expected surprise from them, though, I didn't get it. Frankly, I didn't expect it. On the other hand, they didn't even make a show of asking me who he was.

"You've talked to Delatour?" asked the plumber.

"That's right, can't you tell? Suffice it that it wasn't my idea."

It was around then that I began to realize the plumber wasn't just a plumber. For one thing, he could get around the H in Hadley without making it seem like he was blowing out the candles on a birthday cake. Then there was a kind of deference between the two of them that suggested equality. I mean, the plumbers in France have strictly walk-on, non-speaking parts, and you'll never find a mere police inspector taking over the conversation when his boss is in the room. Also, when the Police Judiciaire want to talk to you, they like the homier atmosphere of the Quai des Orfèvres, whereas Bobet, as his name turned out to be, was sufficiently at home in my hotel suite. In other words, Bobet wasn't Police Judiciaire, and with his next question I could make a fair guess at placing him.

"What do you know about the drug traffic in France, Monsieur?"

For the record, the official name of his branch goes like this: *L'Office Centrale de la Répression du Trafic Illicite de Stupéfiants.* Translated literally, that's The Central Office for the Repression of the Illicit Traffic of Stupefiers. To put it in simple English, Bobet was a nark.

"Come on," I said, grinning lopsidedly at him. "You don't mean to tell me you found some grass in my underpants!"

I guess it wasn't much of a gag. I was the only one grinning, and it hurt me to grin.

The truth was, though, that I didn't know a hell of a lot about the drug traffic in France. From what I'd read and heard, it sounded fairly flourishing, except that latterly the action had begun to play havoc with the balance of payments. By which I mean that if the French narks, with some help from the Americans, had managed to put a lid on the export of the made-in-Marseille varieties, mainly heroin, from an import point of view the joint was as wide open as a slab of Gruyère cheese. And this despite some penalties if you got nailed that made the American statutes look positively permissive.

Bobet largely confirmed this. In fact, to hear him tell it, France was the only country in the world with a dope problem.

"France is a hexagon, Monsieur," he said. "We have three thousand kilometers of land frontiers with six different countries. Four of them are members of the Common Market, which complicates our task immeasurably. Thirty-seven million foreigners visit

France each year. You may enter France by air, sea, train, road, or on foot. We control what we can, when and where we can, but our service is understaffed, and our colleagues in the customs are overworked."

"Well," I said, "I'm sorry to hear that, with all the unemployment too. But if you've got it in mind to offer me a job, I'm afraid I have other plans."

Again, not a smile.

"Under these circumstances," Bobet went on, "we're not interested in the couriers, the street pushers, the middlemen. We can't afford to be. Cut off a branch and the tree continues to grow. Rather it's those at the top we're after, the organizers, the financiers, the..."

"The big bonnets?" I said. "Isn't that what you call them in French."

"The big bonnets, yes. The trouble is that this takes time, time and effort, lengthy investigations which often lead us outside the confines of the hexagon. Unfortunately, our counterparts elsewhere aren't always as cooperative as they might be."

This was the same old song I used to hear in the States: We could close down the dope trade in a week if we only had a little help from —— (Thais) (Turks) (French) (Mexicans) choose one.

"Tell me," I said. "Is Dédé Delatour a big-enough bonnet?"

"For example," Bobet continued, "we know that Grimes was involved in the traffic. We knew it for some time, but we decided not to intervene. We hoped he might lead us further. Now his death has precluded that possibility and complicated the situation."

"By which you mean that Monsieur le Commissaire here needs a murderer?" I glanced at Frèrejean, but if he resented the allusion, he didn't show it. "If so, I've got a pretty solid candidate."

"We also have reason to believe that Hadley was involved," Bobet said, "a conclusion justified by several proven facts in our possession. In addition, they were teammates and they traveled a great deal together, not only inside but outside the hexagon. We even have one specific instance: a flight from Charles de Gaulle to Schiphol Airport, Amsterdam, less than two weeks ago. Grimes and Hadley were known to be carrying a considerable sum of liquid French currency. We know where they took it, and to whom it was paid."

I didn't ask him how they knew, but he made it official by quoting the figures out of a notebook of his own. The sum was indeed considerable.

Bobet put the notebook away and looked at me, dark eyes in a long, lean face.

"The point is this, Monsieur," he said. "We are obliged to move quickly now, and it is imperative that we talk to Hadley. In exchange we are ready, formally, to concede his innocence in the Grimes killing."

"Who is we?"

"Myself and Monsieur le Commissaire Frèrejean, on behalf of our respective services. We are furthermore willing, if we are unable to guarantee total immunity from other prosecution, to take into consideration any cooperation he gives us."

Where I came from, this was called plea bargaining. A tricky business at best, because it puts you in the position of trusting the Law.

"What about other kinds of immunity?" I asked.

"What do you mean?"

"Oh, say from Dédé Delatour, for instance."

The other times I'd mentioned Delatour, the conversation had gone right on. It was obviously a no-no, like farting in public. But this time: silence.

Finally it was Bobet, with a glance at Frèrejean, who broke it:

"All right. Perhaps you had better tell us about your relations with Monsieur Delatour."

"I thought you'd never ask," I said.

I laid it on them then, with all the trimmings. The Glenfiddich helped. I mean, in hindsight I might have hesitated over certain details, because even if the man in question hadn't bragged about it, it would have been obvious that a Mafioso of Delatour's visibility would be plugged into the Law. In Paris, he would virtually have to be. But the forget-me-nots, you could say, were too fresh. I put it all in, then, including Delatour's American connection, and while I was at it, I even offered up the candidacy of Jeannot, the wimp, for the murder of Odessa Grimes. Then, when I was done, I refilled my glass and lifted it in a toast:

"If Delatour isn't a big bonnet in the dope trade, Messieurs, may pure malt whiskey turn to milk."

Again: silence.

Again Bobet, with a glance at Frèrejean, found something to say:

"The drug traffic in France isn't organized by any one person, Monsieur."

Sure, I thought, and you can grow grass in a window box.

"You've made some serious charges, Monsieur," Frèrejean cut in. "Unfortunately, there's not a one of them that would stand up before a court. Now, if Adlay is willing to cooperate with us, we will grant him full police protection."

"Full police protection," I said. "For how long? For the rest of his life?"

"For as long as is necessary."

"And Mlle. Merchadier?"

"Mlle. Merchadier too."

"And what about me?"

"Yourself as well."

I wasn't overly impressed. "You haven't done much of a job of protecting me so far, Monsieur le Commissaire."

"You haven't asked us, Monsieur."

If this was an attempt at irony, you'd never have known it from his expression.

"And you still expect me to be able to deliver Hadley?" I said.

Frèrejean shrugged.

"Don't forget, Monsieur Cage," he said mildly, "you are here in Paris as a guest of France. This is a privilege which can be withdrawn at any moment."

It was an old threat. His colleague Dedini had used it on me before, had even taken me as far as the airport with it. But Dedini had done it with style, gruesome as the style was, whereas Frèrejean came on like pure modern functionaries, with all the gray indifference of their breed.

There it was, in any case. If I could find and produce Roscoe for them, then presumably I could go on living and working in Paris—under "full police protection" to boot. Otherwise it was the airport at Roissy and a one-way ticket—if Delatour didn't get to me first.

Not much of a deal, but there it was.

Bobet, though, had something to add, and I was pretty sure Frèrejean was none too happy about it. Suddenly, in fact, I felt a tension between them.

"We're going to take you into our confidence, Monsieur,"

Bobet said. "We will rely on your discretion. It would be highly damaging to our work if this were known prematurely—by the press, for instance—but our counterparts in Barcelona are holding a man called Atherton, William. He was arrested yesterday, disembarking from an Iberia flight, airport of embarkation: Charles de Gaulle."

"With what?" I said. "Brown sugar in his luggage?"

"Cocaine, Monsieur," he replied dryly. Then he referred to his notebook again. "Atherton, William, born ninth July 1955 at Fresno, California, U.S.A. Nationality: American. Residence permit issued by the Sixième Bureau, Préfecture of Police, Paris. Do you know him, Monsieur?"

"I know the name," I said. "Another basketball player. Wasn't he one of the ones at the P.U.C. gym? When Grimes was killed?"

"No, he wasn't. But he is an athlete by profession, under contract to play professionally for a French sports club."

"Don't tell me who owns the club," I said. "Let me guess."

Again, the farting-in-public reaction.

"Well," I said, "at least your Spanish counterparts, as you call them, are on their toes."

"They arrested Atherton," Bobet replied, "only because we asked them to."

"Oh? And how did you know to ask them?"

At this, Frèrejean started to interrupt, but Bobet waved him off.

"We have our sources of information," he said calmly. "I haven't talked to Atherton yet—I am going to Barcelona this evening—but we are hopeful, under the circumstances, that he will agree to tell us some things we need to know." He closed his notebook. "For reasons I won't go into, it is important we also talk to Hadley. Very important. From his point of view as well. We are counting on you, Monsieur, to convince him of this."

"*If* I can find him," I said.

Neither of them seemed worried about it. Then Bobet stood up, tall and gaunt and with a pointed forehead on which, to my surprise, I could make out small beads of sweat.

Frèrejean was on his feet too.

"We'll be with you at every turn, Monsieur," he told me. "Right beside you. Don't try to elude us this time. You won't succeed. As of this moment, you are under constant surveillance."

"I hope so," I answered.

After they left, I sat down to wait. Maybe that was a funny thing to do when the people who were counting on me on both sides of the Law were already out there beating the bushes, but it was the only idea that came to mind—*under the circumstances,* as Bobet would have said. I opened the windows to air the place out, and I waited, with the Glenfiddich for company, and I made a couple of long-distance calls, which only confirmed what I already knew.

Until, that is, the telephone rang of its own accord, late, and it was time for me to go to the movies.

8

If I've left out the background to those long-distance calls, it's because they added up to nothing. The fact is that even before Odessa Grimes got killed, I'd started fishing the California waters in regard to Roscoe Hadley, or Jimmie Cleever, as he was remembered out there. I'd been handicapped from the start, though, by the loss of my major source of information on the West Coast scene. Freddy Schwartz, a scholarly old rummy of a Jew who'd once worked on the *Times*, had given up the ghost and gone on to hacks' heaven.

Lacking Freddy Schwartz, I'd called two people. One was a private investigator I used to know in Van Nuys who had pretty fair mob connections. The other was a onetime Assistant District Attorney. The onetime Assistant District Attorney had since gone on to better things in Sacramento, but he'd built a political career on the headlines he'd made in the Southland as a "Fearless Young Prosecutor."

Both had left messages while I was a guest at Dédé Delatour's. Now, for want of anything better to do, I called them back. And got the same answer twice: the Jimmie Cleever affair was ancient history, buried by several years' worth of fresher scandals. According to the private eye, the "interested party" we'd talked about couldn't care less about it. Unless, that is, somebody was trying to revive it? Somebody like me, for instance? The onetime Assistant D.A. said he thought the statute of limitations had expired in the Cleever case. There might be ways around that, he agreed, but nobody'd he'd sounded out on the side of the Law, either in Sacramento or Los Angeles, saw potential in reopening it. Unless, that is, I could tie it to something current?

I told them both I'd be in touch. The private eye started to bargain about his fee. I told him to send me a bill.

I'd already gotten the same news through Delatour: nobody in California gave a royal fuck about Roscoe Hadley. This meant that either Roscoe himself had been lying or somebody had sold him a bill of goods. I leaned toward the bill of goods, and for the somebody I voted for Odessa Grimes. The daylight faded into darkness, and I toasted the late Brother Grimes on having won the election. Then I toasted myself for having voted for a winner.

Only why would Brother Grimes have laid the spooks of the past onto his alleged soul- and teammate?

The calls, in any case, proved one thing. I heard the telltale clicking both times, and it wasn't ice cubes, and knowing the Police Judiciaire's predilection for overkill, it wouldn't have surprised me had they plugged into the whole hotel switchboard. So that when the phone rang, several toasts later on, and I picked up the receiver, I answered in English, saying:

"Whoever you are, if you can't be good, be careful. This is a party line."

"*Comment, Monsieur?*" It was the evening hotel operator. She had an incoming call for me.

Who was it? I wanted to know.

The lady wouldn't give her name, the operator said. All she knew was that the call was from outside Paris.

I told her to put it through. Then, when I heard the clicking:

"Be careful what you say, honey chile. Dis heah's a *party* line."

"Is that you, Cage?"

"No, Ma'am. Massah Cage is gone out. Dis is dah butlah speaking."

"What is it, Cage? That's you, isn't it? Have you got someone with you?"

"With me?" I said, in what sounded like my normal voice. More or less. "No, not right now. I'm expecting some of the boys up later for gin rummy. Roscoe said he'd come by, and..."

"For God's sake, are you drunk?"

"Drunk?" I hadn't thought about it that way. I thought about it. "No, I'm not drunk. Just a little fuzzy around the rims."

"Are you all right?"

"Sure I'm all right. The last time I counted, I had two good legs, two good arms. Just one good eye, but who needs two? The nostrils are hanging in there. If you hold on, I'll go count again. All I got is a broken..."

"Stop it, Cage."

"... a broken heart. I guess it's the parties. I guess I've been to too many stag parties lately. I was up all night at Dédé's. You know Dédé Delatour, don't you? He throws a mean party, does Dédé. Too bad you missed it, you'd've had a..."

"I said *stop* it!"

I liked to think I heard hysteria in her voice then. Just a touch, but genuine.

Timed passed. Not a lot of it.

"Are you still there, Cage?"

"I'm still here, baby," I said, semi-soberly.

"Did they hurt you bad?"

"Only when I laughed," I said. "Where are you?"

"It doesn't matter. But tomorrow morning, ten o'clock. I'll be in St. Quentin."

"St. Quentin? Isn't that some kind of cheese?"

"I'm not joking, for God's sake. It's a city."

"Sure it is. Where is it?"

"Look on the map."

"If I've got a map."

"You have a map. Just follow the Autoroute du Nord."

"All right. And how am I supposed to find you when I get there?"

"Look for a white 504." I started to laugh then. Like how many white 504's did she suppose they turned out at Peugeot? "It'll be parked somewhere near the railroad station. Ten o'clock. The license number is 995 BCD 75. Have you got that?"

"I've got it."

"Did you write it down?"

"I don't have to. If I forget, the guys listening in will remind me."

"Never mind that. Repeat it."

I repeated it.

Her voice relaxed then. That was passing strange. Anybody listening in with the right equipment could have long since traced the call, but it didn't seem to bother her. Unless, that is, she was calling from outside the country. She chattered on. She was filled with solicitude about what I was going to do that night. I said I thought I'd go to bed. She said if I went to bed then, I'd be wide awake at three in the morning and nobody to talk to. She said I should take a cold shower, eat a proper meal, and go to the flicks. Hadn't I said I'd never missed a Di Niro flick? She said there was a Di Niro flick playing in the Latin Quarter, original version, I'd have plenty of time for the midnight show if I got started. Then leave a call for eight, and I could make St. Quentin in an hour and a half maximum.

"O.K.?" she said.

"I'll give it some thought," I answered.

There was a moment's pause.

"O.K.," she repeated. Then, in French: *"Je t'embrasse, Cage. A demain."*

I heard a catch in her voice, but I had no way of telling if that was genuine or not.

"I embrace you too, baby," I said in English.

I ran the conversation through after I hung up. Then I checked the movie schedule, took another shower, and washed the excess Glenfiddich out of my pores. Sure enough, *Taxi Driver* was playing again in the Latin Quarter, original version. I'd missed it, first time around. It had gone over big in Paris.

The thing was: I'd never seen a Di Niro flick.

=9=

I got to the theater a little after eleven. It was one of those four-in-one jobs on a little street just off the Boulevard St. Michel. There was no line waiting for *Taxi Driver*. It had turned colder during the day, there was a chill wind swirling papers in the gutters, and, like the lady had said, the next showing was at midnight.

I looked around for a restaurant. There's no shortage in that neighborhood. Every other storefront calls itself one, but the best you can say about them is that theirs is not the cuisine that made France famous. Finally I went into a self-styled Greek joint, meaning mainly that the remains of some animal were turning on a spit in the window. I ordered a steak and French fries, a green salad, and waited for something to happen. Nothing did. The steak and French fries showed up about half an hour later, minus the salad, and in the end I left most of them for the next customer.

Back at the theater, the *Taxi Driver* line had begun to form. I saw nobody I recognized. I got on at the end and became, thereby, part of the captive audience.

Don't get me wrong, I've got nothing against panhandling. I've been stopped on the street and told my share of hard-luck stories, and if the youth of this world are so up against it that they want to try their luck on me, there's at least a chance I'll kick in. But that I should have to listen to their fake Dylan voices for the privilege and their one-chord guitars, well, like they say, there's always TV.

The pair of troubadours working the *Taxi Driver* line were quaint enough as such couples go. The guy had on a thick wool cap pulled down over his ears, a wool sweater that looked like his kid sister might have knitted it, a pair of hugger jeans, and sneakers with no socks. He stamped his feet a lot, though whether to keep time or because of the cold was hard to tell. The girl was a little bit of a waif in a long, shapeless cotton dress and goatskin vest, and at a distance she looked like it was way past her bedtime. Less so, close up. What was quaintest about them, though, was their instruments. The girl's was a recorder. The guy's might have been a recorder too, except that somebody had bent the end of it into a curve. With disastrous results for the tone. I felt like taking up a collection to get them to stop, and put them down mentally for a couple of kids from the sticks who'd decided to try their luck in the big town and needed somebody to tell them they weren't going about it the right way.

Finally the ticket window opened and the line started forward. By this time the guy with the bent recorder was playing alone, bareheaded. The girl was working the line with his cap. When she got to me, I fished in my pocket, annoyed but resigned, and dropped in a franc. Instead of moving on, though, she jammed the cap against my chest.

"I already gave," I said in French.

She glanced up at me briefly and spoke, low but clear, then turned away to the people behind me.

I'd expected some wisecrack about Parisian cheapskates. What I got, though, came out in flat American English.

"When the flick starts," she'd said, "go to the john."

I bought my ticket and went inside. I had a few minutes to think over the pros and cons of it. The lights were on and they were showing some commercials on the screen, like for chocolates that wouldn't melt in your hand, while a couple of usherettes patrolled the aisles with their candy baskets, trying to peddle the stuff. They weren't getting much business. Down in front to the left of the screen were twin doors with a neon sign above, saying: "SORTIE—TOILETTES."

The theater filled up as much as it was going to. The usherettes disappeared with their baskets. I glanced around for people who might have seemed more interested in me than the screen. I didn't spot any. This didn't mean a thing. Then the curtains closed on the commercials, and the lights went out, and then they parted again on the first images of a cabbie weaving through traffic in nighttime New York.

The guy who'd been playing the bent recorder was waiting for me just inside the twin doors. He had his cap back on.

"Follow me," he said, and he took off down a deserted cement corridor.

I ran after him, but he was quicker with his feet than with his instrument. I thought I heard footsteps behind us. The cement corridor forked off into another one, then up a flight of stone steps. I took them two at a time, chased by the image of the Law and Delatour's wimp sprinting behind me, and by the time I got to the top the recorder player had already banged open the metal exit door with his shoulder and was holding it open for me, panting and gesturing.

"You ever ride on one of these things?" he shouted at me.

We came out into the shadows, around the corner from the theater entrance. Parked on the sidewalk was a shining Yamaha 350. The girl who'd been with him before was nowhere in sight.

"Where are the helmets?" I hollered back at him.

"Fuck the helmets!" he answered, and jumping into the saddle, he tromped on the starter. I climbed on behind him, grabbed him around the waist, and off we went in a roar of wind and engine.

The truth is that, back in my ill-spent youth, I'd mucked around with the two-wheelers for a while, but out where I came from the roads were long and mostly straight, and paved with macadam, and you could see the bumps coming up a mile away. Whereas in Paris, half the gutters are still cobbled, and at the intersections that don't have lights it's priority to the right, which means, practically, first come first served. Then too, I'd never ridden behind a death-defying nut like Billy Wheels. He stopped for nothing, moving or stationary, dark or lit, and he gunned at the red lights, and though there was no way we could have been tracked short of helicopters, we were way over on the other side of Boulevard Arago before he deigned to turn on his headlight, and he didn't slow down then either. It was Paris-By-Night all right, but a wild, tire-squealing, squeeze-your-nuts version, with the wind blasting you off your perch and the lights of the night city zooming in on you like flying saucers on a kamikaze run.

We came out somewhere around the Porte de Gentilly. They're building big out that way, and the dark high-risers loomed in on us like tomorrow's dinosaurs. Then it was the Périphérique, the autoroute that circles the city. We went under it, and into the southern suburbs, and quickly I was lost. Totally lost.

Maybe that was the point.

Out beyond the Périphérique, Paris gives way to a ring of what were once small towns—Malakoff, Montrouge, Ivry—but now form an undistinguished magma of warehouses, small industries, and cheap housing, old and new. It's where the onetime Paris proletariat now mostly hangs out, and as nowhere a place as you could hope to find.

Maybe that was the point too.

We wove and swerved through unlit streets, and emerged finally on a block of small one-family houses, known locally as pavilions. My driver slowed, then stopped, and balanced us with one foot in the gutter.

He didn't turn off the engine.

"Here's where you get off," he said over his shoulder.

"What about you?"

"I've got to pick some people up."

Lucky them, I thought.

"Go on," he said, "walk right in. They're waitin' on you."

I got off unsteadily. It was nice to be still alive, but the nerve ends in my pins were jumping like they weren't so sure.

"Who's they?" I called after him.

By then, though, he was already at the corner, and I watched the red of his taillight disappear into the blackness.

The pavilion in question was a small cube of a house with the shutters pulled to and blacker than the suburban night. It was separated from the street by a fence and a narrow yard. The fence had a gate in it. The gate was open. I walked in, through creepers and vines and an undershrubbery that as near as I could tell was mostly garbage. Somewhere a cat yowled, and far off I could hear traffic. Then there was a scurrying in the undergrowth, like I'd disturbed the local night life. And then nothing.

Silence.

I found the front door, listened, hunted for a bell, found none. I knocked. I listened some more. I knocked again, louder.

Nothing.

Maybe it was a surprise party.

I gave the doorknob a twist and a push.

The door gave, reluctantly at first.

I walked into a hallway. The hallway was dark, empty, but light diffused dimly out of an adjoining room. It came from a single bulb in the ceiling, but the bulb had been wrapped around with cloth and all that got through was a weak purplish glow. I could see layers of smoke hovering, immobile, in the glow. They were as thick as in the basement smoker of the old Yakima Elks Club, only the Yakima Elks never lit up stuff like this. The smell was thick, acrid, pungent, like grass burning on a prairie. You had a choice between a free high and asphyxiation.

I made out clumps and humps on the floor under the lowest layer of smoke. At first I took them for cushions, but they were human all right, single and clustered, frozen into the postures of the sleeping or the stoned. Then one of them stirred at my feet, a bent one that was held in place by the junction of floor and wall. It lifted a head, pointed an arm in a vague gesture.

"In there," it said.

"In where?" I answered, my voice suddenly loud. This set off a stirring among the clumps, but the one that had directed me sank back into never-never land.

Across the room, I could pick out a thin pencil line of yellow light at floor level, with the outline of a door above it. I made my way over, careful to avoid stepping on the heads.

The bright light of the second room set my eyes to blinking. Apparently it had been the kitchen, back in the days when kitchens doubled as family rooms. And maybe it still was, because there was an old-style single sink in a corner, plus a cooker and sawed-off refrigerator, both old models. There were dishes in the sink too. But the homiest touch of all, in the junk and clutter, were two more

Yamahas parked against the far wall.

In the center of the room, under the ceiling globe, was a big oval wood table that had seen better days. It was strewn with papers, some of them weighted by what looked like a toolbox.

Sitting behind the table, his glasses up in his hair, his head down, was one Robert H. Goldstein, better known to me as Bobby H.

"Better close the door, Cage, and sit down," said Bobby H. He didn't look up. "I'll be with you in a second. Help yourself if you smoke the stuff. It's Dutch grade."

He had a pocket calculator out on the table next to him and punched figures into it from small slips of paper, then transcribed the results into a long cardboard-bound ledger, then crumpled the slips of paper and dropped them onto the floor. On my side of the table were the remains of a loaf of hash about the size of a brick. It had been wrapped in aluminum foil, remnants of which were still folded over the end of it.

"Or stand up if you want," said Bobby H., concentrating on his work.

I pulled out a chair and sat down. There was something about him that affected me that way. I took out my tobacco pouch, stuffed a pipe and lit up. He wrinkled his nose at the smoke. Later on, he said something to the effect that tobacco could kill you.

He looked about the same as the last time I'd seen him, a skinny Jewish kid with freckles and tired eyes. He had on the same neckless baseball shirt, with a red-and-black lumberjack over it. I knew he was twenty-four, but any law-shy saloonkeeper would have asked him for proof of his age.

"I hear my old man's upped the ante on me again," he said, still not looking up.

I didn't say anything. I wondered idly how he knew.

"I talked to him, you know? I called the mother up. Like it was his birthday."

He finished with the last of his slips, crumpled and dropped it, then pushed some papers together and piled them on top of the toolbox, then the ledger on top of the papers.

"The mother can't accept the idea that I'm making a bigger profit than he is."

"What's all that?" I asked, gesturing at the pile. "Toting up the day's take?"

"Not just the day's," he said with a laugh. "You let the paperwork pile up, it... But *hey!*"

He'd just glanced at me. Now he adjusted his glasses and took a closer look.

"Hey, man, you know you look like somebody's been working you over with a pick and a shovel?"

"That's not far from it."

"Holy shit! Who did it?"

"Never mind. Besides, you didn't go to all the trouble of hauling me out here just to commiserate."

"Trouble? It's no trouble. Like we do it all the time."

"Sure, and what's your accident rate?"

He didn't get that at first. Then he laughed enthusiastically.

"You talking about Billy Wheels? He's a mother on a bike, honh? He doesn't have a broken bone in his body, you know? Not that I'd ride with him on a bet!"

It was a nice time for him to tell me.

"Look, man," he went on, "the thing is this, you know? I want to get this bullshit with my old man straightened out once and for all. I don't have the time to hassle with him. You know what the mother wants? He wants me to come back and learn the business.

Books, man, isn't that the *pits?* The total *pits?* In five years, he says, I'll be a vice-president, in ten years he's retiring and it'll all be mine. Shit, man, *I'm* the one who's going to be retiring, and in a lot less than ten years!"

He paused, for effect.

"Business is that good?" I asked.

"*That good?* Are you putting me on? Hash is the biggest growth product in France, man. We've only begun to touch the market, only *begun!* It's a *volume* market out there, all it wants is price and product, and that's what we're giving them. Shit, that stuff you see there, you figure it out. That's grade hash, man. Sells for two francs a gram in Amsterdam if you can buy volume. When it gets out on the street here, it goes for anywhere from ten to twelve depending. A little cheaper in Paris, you know? A little higher outside? Translate that into kilos, you'll see the kind of margins we're operating on. But we're talking about *tons*, man! Fucking *tons!* And no advertising, low overhead."

"What about the competition?"

"The competition? The hell you say. This isn't like the States, man, it's wide open! Sure there're other people selling hash in Paris, we know them, they know us. But they can't get near the market like we can, not when it comes to hash. Shit, they try to sell *us* the stuff! Wholesale, you know? And sometimes we buy it, depending. But you got to be careful, you know? Buying in Paris. People here are packing horseshit, literally, and selling it for Dutch grade."

"People like Dédé Delatour?"

"Delatour's a total jerk-off, you know? So is Loulou. But that's where it's at, man, don't you see? You want me to let you in on the secret?"

"Yeah, Bobby," I said, "why don't you do that?"

—95—

He didn't need encouragement from me, though. He was only warming to his subject.

"It's one product, man. One product. You find one quality product that the public wants, you bring it to them at a fair price with a big margin, you keep your overhead down, and *that's* where it's at. That's where what they teach you in business school is so much bullshit, you know? Diversify, they say, conglomerates, spread out the risk. Total bullshit. You take my old man, he's in book publishing, right? And he does pretty well, right? So you know what he just did with the profits? He bought an amusement park! In Florida, man! A fucking amusement park, you know? Now, what does he know about Ferris wheels? Not a goddam thing. So he's going to have to hire a team of high-priced executives to run it for him, right, and before he knows it, his overhead's going to go right through the fucking roof! Isn't that the pits? We deal in one product, man. Hash, quality grade. We won't even touch the heavy stuff. People are trying to sell it to us all the time, you know? Shit, some of our customers are screaming for it! But let them get it elsewhere, I don't care. Simplify, that's the secret! Not diversify, totally *simplify!* If the people ever stop smoking hash, like we'll go out of business, that's all. You take the bookkeeping, you know? You know what our bookkeeping consists of? One book, man. Simple. It's all right here, every transaction. Go ahead, take a look."

He took the cardboard ledger off the pile and slung it over to my side of the table.

"What about the Law?" I said.

"Well, what about them? They've got to catch us first, man. We travel light, you know? By the time you leave here, we'll be packing up, moving on. Tomorrow night we'll be some place else, and the night after that. Sure, every so often they nail somebody, the distributors mostly. But what're they going to do? It's like this, man: did you ever read Borges?"

"Who?"

"Borges. Jorge Luis Borges, you know? Anyway, he wrote a story about a bunch of cartographers. Mapmakers? They've been assigned to make a new map of their country. Except that they're so hung up on getting every last total detail of the country onto the map that they end up making a map as big as the country itself! You get it? It's a paradox, you know? But that's what they'd have to do to suppress hash: arrest every man, woman, and child under thirty in all fucking France. Total arrest, man. The whole population!"

"I see what you mean," I said. "But suppose they arrested *you?*"

"So? So somebody else takes over. Like I already got mine stashed away. What comes in now is just frosting on the cake."

"You might have to wait a few years to get it."

"I doubt that."

"Do you? From what I hear, the penalties in France are pretty stiff. They can lock you up and throw away the key."

"Not in my case."

"Oh? Why's that?"

He grinned and, propping his glasses back up on his head, stretched out his arms.

"Because if worst comes to worst, Cage, my old man'll get me off, you know? Or hire somebody like you to do it for him."

What I've put down here wasn't the half of it. As it turned out, we had a long wait, and, like most Jews, Bobby H. couldn't resist the chance to show off how sharp he was. From what he said, I got the feeling the product counted less for him than the action. I mean, he could as well have been peddling yarmelkes to the Eskimos. It was a tradition as old as Moses, and you knew too that if things ever went wrong and the bottom fell out of the skullcap trade, you'd hear him shouting anti-Semitism all the way to the bank.

At some point he took the toolbox off the pile of papers and opened it up. It was one of those models that have the little divided trays on top for the screws and washers, with the big stuff underneath. Only in this case, when he lifted out the tray, the big stuff was all cash. It ranged from ten-franc notes on up. He fished around till he'd come up with ten five-hundred-franc jobs. He squared them into a pile, then counted them like a bank teller, then pinned them together French-style and tossed them across the table toward me. This was just a down payment, he said. There'd be the same each week, cash, for as long as necessary. It was for me to keep his old man happy, and if I couldn't keep him happy, then at least off his back. Because he was tired of all the bullshit and he had better things to worry about.

I let the money lie there, next to the cardboard ledger. It was still lying there when we heard the sound of a motor out in the street. It was a two-wheeler all right.

"That'll be them," said Bobby H. "It's about time. Three fucking hours. You sit tight, man, I'll go get them." He went out a back door. A minute or two later he was back, followed by a woman I'd never seen before, followed by my onetime chauffeur, Billy Wheels, followed by the little waif in the long dress. I didn't know how they'd made it, three on a bike, but their faces were red and they were blowing hard. Between them, Billy Wheels and the waif lifted the Yamaha over the doorsill and parked it against the back wall, next to the others.

The woman had on a navy-blue cloth coat with the collar up. Her hair was black, curly, and streaked with gray. The gray, I guessed, might have been premature. She looked out of place in that kitchen. For a couple of seconds, though, I thought that was just the contrast between her get-up and the surroundings.

"We're late," said Billy Wheels, catching his breath. "Man, we had a bitchin' time making the connection."

"Poor Cage," said Valérie, taking off the wig and shaking her hair out. "They really worked you over, didn't they. *Les salauds*. Here, let me see."

10

Normally you can make Paris-Brussels in three hours by the Autoroute du Nord and not even work up a sweat. But we were on the road twice that long the next day. For one thing, we stayed off the Autoroute du Nord, and for a long stretch after Reims and up through the Ardennes we weren't on any autoroute at all. Then too, we weren't going to Brussels.

Not even to Belgium, except to pass through.

That was only something she'd said for Bobby H.'s benefit.

She'd said a lot of things for Bobby H.'s benefit. She'd put on quite a show. By the time she was done, the coffee had been brewed, the sky was growing light, and some of the other members of the Hash Collective had come stumbling out of the next room, looking for empty cups. She had Bobby H.'s five thousand francs in her purse, and there was a VW Beetle parked out in front of the house. The Beetle was for us. It had seen better days, but it had German plates and rental papers made out to yours truly. Bobby H. had worked it out with a garage in Montrouge, and Billy Wheels had gone to pick it up for us.

She kissed Bobby goodbye. A tender clinch, even touching. Then we drove off, under a swollen gray sky that didn't look like it would brighten much, and Valérie said to me:

"Any time you want now, Cage."

"Any time I want what?"

"Out," she said. "Any time you want, you can stop the car and get out."

I glanced at her. She had the wig back on, and the frumpy coat, and she didn't look like she'd last till the first toll booth.

"What makes you think I want out?" I said.

"I could read it in your face. The minute I walked in last night. The way you stared at me."

"Stared at you?"

"That's right."

"But that was only my natural loving expression, baby."

She didn't answer. Her mouth went tight and her eyes fixed on the windshield.

I shook my head.

"No way," I said. "It's too much fun. It's not every day I get to spend the night tied to a chair and have my face scrambled. Hell, now I've got half of Paris looking for me. I'm having a ball. What's more, it's all for free."

"You blame it on me too, don't you?"

"In a way," I said. "The way I figure it, you got me in, now you're going to get me out. The only way out is Roscoe, and that's where we're going now, isn't that right? Unless, that is, you want to tell me where to find him myself. In which case, *you* could be the one to get out."

You never know. Maybe I laid it on a little thick. Maybe she was already strung out from having crossed half the map of Europe since I'd seen her last. In other words, maybe the tears staining her cheeks were genuine enough.

At least they were quieter than the last time.

Around about then I spotted a filling station. I pulled in next to the pumps. She got out and headed for the toilets. I watched her go, while the gas jockey filled up the Beetle. When she came back, the wig was gone and she'd worked some on her face. It helped. She still didn't look, though, like she'd last till the first toll booth.

"We're in it together, then?" she said.

"It looks that way."

"O.K. Then let me tell you what happened."

"Later. Catch some sleep first."

She shook her head.

"I need to talk now," she said.

"O.K.," I said, turning the key in the ignition. "Talk now."

She did too, some fifteen minutes' worth, before her eyes closed and she nodded off. I turned on the car radio. Later on, when she woke up, we talked some more. It had started to rain. The she took over the driving and I caught some sleep. The way it worked out, we had plenty of time for all of it: driving, sleeping, talking, working the windshield wipers. Even listening to the radio. Which turned out to be pretty important too.

After I'd left them at the Neuilly apartment, she and Roscoe had had it out. Roscoe hadn't lied to us because of her or Marie-Josèphe Lamentin. Marie-Josèphe, he'd told her, was just something that had happened. But it was me, he'd said. He didn't trust me, never had. Number one: I was a honkie. Number two: I knew Johnny Vee. Number three: I struck him like the kind of honkie who'd sell his mother if the price was right.

At which Valérie had blown her stack. If that was how he really felt, she'd told him, then he could count her out too.

At which Roscoe had said that he was through lying, that if I could fix up his alibi with Marie-Josèphe he wasn't going to mistrust me any more, and he swore it, and then Valérie had gone out to buy food and spotted the stake-out sitting in a white 504 across the street.

She hadn't known who he was, she said. But when he followed her, she figured there was more to be gained by inviting him up than pretending to ignore him. So she'd invited him up.

Back in the apartment, Roscoe had played possum at first. It was only when the stake-out started helping Valérie lay out the food that he made his move. One grab and he had his gun arm, then his gun, then the scruff of his neck.

Roscoe had shaken it out of him that he worked for Delatour. Delatour, Roscoe knew, was Johnny Vee's French connection. The stake-out claimed not to know anything about that. He claimed too not to know why Delatour wanted them watched, only that he was supposed to report in once every hour.

This left them with a choice to make, and little time to make it in. If Delatour was on to them, the chances were he was also on to me. Conceivably I was walking into a trap, but it was already too late to warn me. Furthermore, the Neuilly apartment was blown, they had no other place to fall back on.

In the end, hoping that I could fend for myself, they decided to take off.

They drove as far as St. Quentin in the stake-out's car, and, as far as she knew, it was still there where they'd abandoned it two days ago. Because if the police were checking the frontiers, then probably, she'd figured, they'd stand a better chance crossing on the train. In St. Quentin they'd gotten on the Paris-Amsterdam express. The train was crowded, and when it reached the border, she made Roscoe lock himself in the toilet cubicle while she powdered her nose in the mirror. The check was only perfunctory. They got through.

Amsterdam was Roscoe's idea. He knew some bloods there who

would help them. It was night, though, when they arrived, they didn't find the bloods till the next morning, finally they spent what was left of the night in an awful fleabag on the Damrak while she called all over Paris—frantically, she said—trying to find out what had happened to me. The next morning—that was yesterday—they'd managed to track down one of the bloods, an itinerant basketball player called Wallace Edner. This was in a saloon off the Zeedijk. Roscoe went in with his palms up, expecting a great old reunion. Instead they got the fish eye. Wallace Edner wasn't about to do anything for Brother Roscoe. In fact, all they learned from him was that the word was out: Brother Roscoe was untouchable.

Roscoe's notion at this point was to get back on the train and go. Any train anywhere, as far as the money would take him. Would take *him*, mind you. Because Valérie had done enough for him, it was time for her to get off and for him to do his disappearing number again. Like history repeating itself. Alone.

Only Valérie wouldn't buy it. Apparently they'd had quite a scene. In the end it had meant, as she put it, that she had to open a drawer of her life that she'd as soon have kept closed, but the important thing was that now she had Roscoe in a safe place. She couldn't keep him there forever, but long enough to come get me.

Which, with the help of a credit card, a rented car, and Bobby H., she'd managed to do.

It was a nice story, all in all. It even had its poignant moments. Killjoy that I am, though, I had to go and pick some holes in it.

"Why didn't you?" I said.

"Why didn't I what?"

"Why didn't you let him get on the next train and do his disappearing number?"

She glanced at me. She was driving by this time, talking while she drove. I admired her style behind the wheel.

"I'm not like that, Cage," she said.

"Yeah. It's too bad, though, in a way. I mean, look at us right now. We've got your credit card, we've got my credit card, we've got wheels. We've even got Bobby's five thousand francs. Between us we could see a lot of Europe before winter."

She said that was a beautiful idea. Someday, she said, we were going to do it. She wasn't going to let me forget.

"Don't," I said. "But suppose then we try another idea on for size. Just supposing it turned out that nobody was out for Roscoe's skin."

"What do you mean by that?"

"Just what I say. Johnny Vee, for instance, and the rest of the California mob. Supposing they couldn't care less what happened to Roscoe Hadley."

She thought about it.

"I don't get it," she said, shaking her head. "Unless it's your day for bad jokes."

"Bad or not," I said, "this joke happens to be true."

She didn't look at me, but I could see her knuckles blanch on the steering wheel.

"How do you know it's true?"

"I've checked it out. Several ways."

"Are you sure?"

"Yeah. I'm sure."

She thought about that too, and I watched her think. She flicked on the left blinker, then pulled out to pass a truck, then veered back into the righthand lane.

She shook her head. Slowly.

"I find it hard to believe," she said.

"Why?"

"I don't think he's that good an actor. Roscoe, I mean. Oh, he's good. But not with me."

"That's what I'd have thought," I said. "But it doesn't mean—necessarily—that Roscoe's been acting."

"Oh?"

"He could have been genuinely scared. He could have thought they really did have a contract out on him. In fact, I think he did." I paused. "In that case, though, then somebody did a mighty good job of convincing him."

She didn't say anything straight off. She drove. She kept her hands on the wheel and her eyes straight out through the wipers.

"Who?" she said tensely.

"Well, it's pretty obvious, isn't it? Didn't Roscoe as much as tell us himself? It was Brother Odessa. It had to be."

I was watching her carefully. Maybe she relaxed a little; maybe she didn't.

"But I also thought," I added, "that it might have been you."

It's a risky business to spring things on people when they're driving in the rain at 120 kilometers an hour. I mean, you could get killed that way. At that, what kept us from it may have been only that there wasn't another car on that immediate stretch of Route Nationale. Even so, the Beetle swerved drastically off the road onto the shoulder, then jerked back with a shudder, and our ass end skidded sideways in the wet and out into the oncoming lanes.

Valérie fought with the wheel. We swerved back, in a blinding spray of mist. A moment later we were back on our own side and charging up the highway. Some fifty meters farther on, though, she eased off on the accelerator. Then she pulled off the road and stopped.

Her hands were shaking.

"All *right!*" she said, glaring at me. Her eyes were dry but small and pointed with anger. "Let's have the rest of it. *Out* with it! *All* of it!"

"All of what?"

"I didn't convince Roscoe of *anything!* I didn't set him up for *anything!* If he was taken in by Odessa, then I was too! But you obviously think otherwise, and if you think otherwise about that, then you obviously think otherwise about a lot of other things!"

"Maybe I'm just the suspicious type," I said.

It didn't much matter, though, what I said right then. She was off and running, working herself up as she went, and there was no stopping her. There never is, with the good ones. Finally it wasn't just me and my suspicious nature, it was my gender, ancestry, race, species, all the way back to the unlucky stiff who planted the first apple tree.

It was something to experience all right. Her eyes blazed, her body arched, and the very air crackled with her anger. But it was pretty clear too that if I'd asked the wrong question, I'd touched the right nerve.

The storm died down, as storms will.

She lit a cigarette, then stubbed it out. Then lit another one. This one stayed lit.

"O.K.," I said, "let's do it your way. Out with it. Cards on the table. Right?"

"All right."

"Then let's start with Dédé Delatour."

She bit at her upper lip.

"He's a *salaud*, Cage," she said tersely. She'd called me that too, in her run-down on my character, but, the French language being short on obscenity, *salaud* has to cover the whole gamut from louse to mother-raper.

"So I found out," I said. "He spoke very highly of you too."

"What did he say?"

"He called you a resourceful bitch, among other things. I got the impression you know each other pretty well."

She looked away.

"We did," she said. "Once. It was through him, in fact, that... all right, that I met Roscoe. The trouble with Dédé is that he likes to think he owns people. Like toys. When it doesn't work out that way, he's like a child."

"A child? Pretty vicious for a child, if you ask me."

"Children can be vicious too."

"And naïve?"

"Naïve?" she said questioningly. "In what way?"

"Well, I spent a pretty bad night, courtesy of Dédé Delatour. There was one thing, though, that I still can't figure out. From the minute I met him, he had me pegged as the hit man who'd been assigned to Roscoe. I was supposed to get Roscoe, and he couldn't understand what was taking me so long. He was so sure of it, he hadn't even bothered to check it out. Now, doesn't that sound pretty naïve?"

She was working at the lip again.

"All right," she said tersely. "I told him."

"You told him what?"

"That you'd been hired to get Roscoe."

"Jesus Christ!"

"I had to, Cage. He wanted to know what you were doing, hanging around Roscoe."

"And he believed you?"

"He had every reason to. I'd already been to him before. When I first found out Roscoe was in trouble. I went to see him. I told him the whole story. I begged him to stop it."

"And what did he say?"

"He said there wasn't anything he could do, not even if he wanted to. He said his relationship with the people in America was entirely business, that he couldn't intervene. Besides..."

She faltered, then caught herself.

"He laughed at me," she said flatly. "He said it would be good for me. That it would teach me a lesson."

I could picture the scene. I didn't much enjoy it.

"So when Delatour turned you down, you went job-hunting?"

"That's right."

"And came to me?"

"Yes."

"And after that you told him I was the hit man from California?"

"Yes."

"Jesus H. Christ," I said. "Didn't it occur to you that he could check it out just by picking up the telephone?"

"It occurred to me. But I didn't think he would."

"Oh? Why not?"

"For one thing, I can be persuasive. For another..."

"For another?"

She sucked air again, and her lips went white, but she kept her eyes on mine.

"There were things going on that he didn't want them to know about."

"Ahhh. Like what kinds of things?"

"Drugs," she said. "As far as the California people knew, it was just basketball."

"You mean the players he was hiring from Johnny Vee were doing a little moonlighting off the court and he didn't want Johnny Vee to know it?"

"What's moonlighting?"

I explained.

"That's right," she said. "Some of them were. They traveled a lot, they made a lot of money at it." She shrugged. "It was easy money. No one got caught."

"What about Roscoe?"

"No," she said sharply. "That was just the point. Roscoe didn't want any part of it. He knew it was going on, but he'd always refused. That was one reason Dédé wouldn't lift a finger for him."

"I think you're wrong."

"I'm *not* wrong," she insisted.

"Maybe he didn't do it for Delatour," I said. "But he did for Odessa."

"I don't believe you."

"You don't have to."

I told her about Bobet then, and what he'd said. She took the news hard. This surprised me. I mean, she'd been around enough, I'd have thought, not to have too many illusions left. I even found myself defending Roscoe to her. Odessa Grimes may have started out moonlighting for Delatour, but the way it looked to me, he'd branched off into business for himself. And having done so, he'd recruited Roscoe by the sweetest kind of shakedown: (1) Johnny Vee had a contract out for him; (2) he, Odessa, was going to protect him against all comers; (3) therefore he, Roscoe, owed Odessa a small favor or two, like carrying some stuff around for him in his hand luggage. Then, when Odessa had gotten sliced, it was no wonder Roscoe had started jumping at shadows. Had he been there, chances were he'd have gotten it too. Furthermore, the murder had Jeannot's signature written all over it, so that when the stake-out Valérie had lured into the Neuilly apartment turned out to be another of Delatour's hands, there'd been nothing left for Roscoe to do but run like hell.

This was, I thought, a pretty fair piece of analysis. It plugged up most of the holes, and all of them as far as Valérie was concerned. But it was wrong in one important respect, and if I'd realized it then, maybe I'd have managed to convince her to take that Grand Tour of Europe then and there.

Instead, I reached across her.

She put her hand on my arm.

"Please, Cage," she said. "I can't drive any more. Not right now."

"You don't have to," I said. "Right now I just want to listen to the news."

I'd caught the tail end of the bulletins the previous hour, while she was sleeping. I hadn't been paying attention at first, and I'd missed most of it. Now we heard it all. It was a testament to something or other, I suppose, that the still-unsolved murder of the black American basketball star had been shoved back near the weather report. As far as that went, the police were still looking for one Roscoe Hadley and following up numerous leads. But the French police, narcotics division, were also questioning another basketball player, also black, also American, who was being held in Barcelona, Spain, on a charge of transporting drugs. L'Office Centrale de la Répression du Trafic Illicite des Stupéfiants was maintaining an official silence concerning the affair, but, according to informed speculation, the athlete in question was part of a dope-smuggling ring.

So much, I thought, for Bobet's "in strictest confidence."

Even this story, though, had been pushed aside by a more sensational event. According to the announcer, Paris hadn't known a night like the night before since the worst underworld wars of the fifties. Shortly after midnight, when Montmartre was at its liveliest, a group of unidentified gunmen had literally invaded a well-known café and brasserie on Place Clichy and, before the terrorized eyes of the numerous clientèle and staff, had brazenly shot and killed four men and gravely wounded two others. The six victims, all of whom had been identified, were known to have underworld connections. The brasserie had been sealed, and the Anti-Gang Brigade of the Paris police had been called in to spearhead the investigation.

"It's a wonder," I said, "that they've got anybody left to look for us."

"Who?"

"The Paris Law. Do you know any of the victims?"

"No."

"Never heard of any of them?"

She hadn't. Neither had I. Probably they weren't Delatour's. On the other hand, it could have been Delatour's who'd done the shooting.

There was the weather too. It was raining everywhere in France, the announcer said, except on the Côte d'Azur. A low-pressure zone had extended over the continent from the Atlantic, and the rain was expected to continue all day, with average temperatures dropping below the seasonal norms.

I switched the radio off. We sat there, listening to the rain plip-plipping on the Beetle's roof. Every so often a car went by, spraying us with water. Nobody paid us any mind.

"Cards on the table," Valérie said. "I've told you everything, Cage. There's nothing left out."

"O.K.," I said, my hand on the door handle. "I'm going to drive now. We'd better get going."

"There's just one thing," she said, reaching toward me.

She was smiling, around the eyes as well as the mouth. Her tongue licked across her upper lip.

It was like her, I realized, to up the ante when you least expected it.

"I want to fuck you," she said.

"Now? Here?"

"Now. Here."

An improbable proposition. I mean: a rain-swept road in the middle of nowhere, a rented Beetle with a stick shift on the floor, and she having just made a confession which, as far as I could tell, had cost her.

I grinned at her.

"That's a beautiful idea too," I said. "And I won't let you forget it either. Right now, though, I think we'd better go talk to Brother Roscoe."

=11=

We went out of France at the corner of the Belgian border where the little duchy of Luxembourg tucks into the picture. This was a tip from Bobby H., in case anyone was looking for us, and, what with the weather, it turned out to be a good one. The last representative of the French Republic didn't so much as come out of his booth to say hello. He just looked up and motioned us through.

We picked up the autoroute again near Liège and rolled across Belgium without stopping. Which was just as well. From what I've seen of it, the land of the Walloons and the Flemings is a bastard place, half French and half Dutch, with the best of each left out. But Holland is something else, and if Holland is something else, then Amsterdam, friend, is one of the last of the great towns. The travel hucksters like to call it the Venice of the North, but according to Cage's Pleasure Guide to the Old Continent, the Venetians would have to work a hundred years to make their town as civilized as the inner city of the burghers.

As it happened, though, we didn't get near enough to Amsterdam that day to wave. We were headed for a pocket-sized Dutch fairyland to the south of it, off the road to The Hague and the North Sea resort of Scheveningen. I call it a fairyland simply because it's hard to believe people still live in places like that. I mean private citizens like you and me. I know some of the French châteaux are still inhabited, and Nico van den Luyken's domain could have fit into a corner, say, of Vaux-le-Vicomte. But the French châteaux-dwellers—the two-legged ones, that is—are, for the most part, doddering aristocrats who live in one room because that's all they can afford to heat, whereas Nico van den Luyken's domain included a functioning windmill, expanses of orchard, a model dairy farm, and a stone-and-brick manse that, even in the rain, put the third little pig to shame.

To top it all off, he ran the joint at a profit.

I've said that Valérie had had to reopen a drawer of her life on Roscoe's account. The drawer, apparently, contained Nicolas van den Luyken. The image is wrong, though. Nico van den Luyken would have taken up the whole cupboard. He was a tall, ruddy, and efficient-looking Dutchman with a shock of auburn hair speckled with gray and beard to match, plus a grip you weren't about to forget. He spoke impeccable English. He had the self-assured manner of his class and surroundings that made you feel like you'd somehow missed the boat. He was discreet about it, though, to the point that once he'd seen to it that we had a bath, fresh clothes, and a drink, he left us alone with Roscoe, saying only that dinner would be served whenever we wanted it.

When I came downstairs, I found Roscoe alone in Nico's living room. He didn't fit the image either, at least not the one I'd formed mentally. He was sprawled in a low couch, a tumbler of orange juice beside him, with his legs stretched out toward a crackling fire, and reading the European edition of *Newsweek* under an arching stainless-steel lamp. The threads he had on were Nico's, and they fit him amazingly well: pressed flannel trousers, a thick natural-wool turtleneck, and a hound's-tooth tweed jacket that had a Bond Street look. The only anachronism was his footgear: Adidas sneakers, white with blue stripes. The sartorial resources of the estate, I guessed, didn't go as far as Roscoe's shoe size. But, beholding him, a Martian touring the Earth for the first time could only have said: "What's that you were telling me about the oppressed black peoples?"

"Hey there," said Roscoe when I came in. He gave me a wave. "Come on in out of the rain, stranger, dry your feets and tell us the news from down home."

"The news from down home," I said, "is that they've started shooting at each other in the streets."

"In *Paris?* I'd've ... But hey, man! You look like you been catching some of that shit yourself!"

"So I did," I said. "But that was before they started with live ammunition."

He whistled, puffing his cheeks.

"Sounds to me like a good place to stay away from," he said. Then he dropped the magazine and, reaching out both arms behind him, stretched like an elongated cat. He yawned deeply. "Must be getting *warm* in here. The fire makes me sleepy. Seems like all I done here is *sleep*, man. Shoot, if I wasn't such a lazy nigger, I'd get up and have off this coat." He chuckled. "Well, come on, man. Aren't you going to tell me who's after my ass today?"

"Not so many people as you'd think."

"No? Well, that's depressing news. I guess I must be losin' my touch."

I started to tell him about the Law and Delatour, but then van den Luyken and Valérie came in. Our host busied himself at the bar. He didn't have Glenfiddich, he told me, but if I fancied the pure malts, wouldn't I sample his own brand? I would, and did, and we drank a toast of appreciation to the Highland distillers. Then he asked if there was anything else we needed. I wanted to see the day's papers from Paris. He replied, a little ruefully, that it was too late for him to do anything about it then, but that we'd have them at breakfast. At which, glass in hand, he left us alone.

"Did you tell him yet?" Valérie asked me.

"Tell me what yet?" said Roscoe.

"We were just getting there," I answered. "But first off, Roscoe, let me ask you something. Your old friends in California, you know—Mr. Vee and his fellow sportsmen?—how was it you first found out they were onto you again?"

"First found out?" He laughed at that, then, when I didn't join him, stared at me big-eyed. "Man, they *always* been after my ass! I been *shot* at! When I was down in Mexico, some blood pulled a gun on me, tried to shoot my fucking head off. The bullet went right past my *ear!* You ever hear a bullet go right past your *ear?*"

He made a flat, whistling sound.

"I'm not talking about Mexico," I said. "I'm talking about Paris."

"Paris, yeah. Mexico, Paris, what difference does it make? You name the place, man, I *been* there."

"But there was a long time in between, wasn't there? Between Mexico and Paris?"

"That's right. Three, four years."

"During which things cooled down?"

"I don' know about that. There's things that never cool down."

"But enough for you to start playing ball again?"

"I took the chance, man."

"O.K. Now, who was it who told you in Paris that they were onto you again?"

"Like nobody had to *tell* me, man. That was something *knowed.*"

There was something in his speech I'd noticed before: when he felt the squeeze coming on, his talk went nigger, complete with leaning on the verbs.

"But somebody did tell you, didn't he? Didn't Odessa tell you?"

"Odessa *knew* 'bout it, sure. But so did the other bloods. You don' under*stan*', man. We got the grapevine. Things like that get around."

"Sure they do. But they get around because somebody starts them. Didn't Odessa start this one?"

"You don' understan', man. Nobody *started* it. It..."

"That's not what you said," Valérie cut in impatiently. "You said it was Odessa who told you about it. You said if it ever got out that he'd told you, his own head would be on the block. You even said that was what friends were all about."

"Did I say that?" His eyes were big again, with white and innocence.

"You certainly did."

"Well, maybe I did. But so what? Odessa only got it from some place else."

"No," I said, "that's where you're wrong. He didn't get it from some place else. He's where it started."

"Now what in hell would...?"

His voice trailed off.

"He lied," Valérie said. "Nobody was out to get you, at least nobody from California. Cage has verified it. Without wanting to, he even got Dédé to verify it."

Roscoe looked at me.

"That's the way it checks out," I said. "As far as Johnny Vee's concerned, you're ancient history. I'm not saying that if you went home, you'd get met at the airport with a brass band, but as long as you stay over here, they're not going to hassle you."

I guess you don't run scared for years and then shake the hand of the man who tells you there's nothing to be afraid of. The more so if you're black and the man who's bringing you the news is white. In other words, I didn't expect gratitude from him.

He didn't disappoint me either.

"Why *would* Odessa have done that?" said Valérie.

"I don't know that he did," Roscoe answered sharply. "It's Cage's word against him."

"He played you for a fool," she went on. "You know it too. He was dealing in drugs, and he wasn't the only one. They wanted you to join in. You told me about that too, remember? How they were after you all the time but you didn't want to get messed up in it?"

"That's the truth. I sure didn't want to get messed up with dope."

"Then why did you?" I asked.

"I..."

"Wait a minute," Valérie interrupted. "It was Dédé's business too, remember? But you said you didn't owe him anything. He hadn't brought you into the league, he hadn't signed you up. Isn't that right?"

"That's right. I didn't owe Delatour nothin'."

"Whereas you did Odessa?"

"Odessa was my friend, sure, but..."

"We know who killed him, Roscoe," she said. "It was one of Delatour's hoodlums. We know why too. They'd have killed you too, for the same reason, if they hadn't thought that was Cage's job."

"*Cage's* job? Now, what the hell you *talkin'* about?"

She laid it on him, how she'd told Delatour I was the hired gun from California, and why. He whistled again, blowing hard through his cheeks.

"Honey," he said, "you were takin' some hell of a *chance*."

"That's not the point," she said flatly. "The point is that you and Odessa were dealing together."

"Now, hold it there! *Hold* it! I. . . ."

"Delatour's not the only one who knows," I said. "The Law does too."

"*What* Law?"

It was my turn to explain, about Bobet and the conversation we'd had, and the file the narks already had going on him. I watched him squirm with it. He squirmed all right, all six-feet-seven of him, and grabbed his hair, and blew wind through his cheeks, and he said that, between me and Val and Delatour and the Law, it was the same old story, the white folks ganging up on the niggers again. But in the end, that phony air of injury and disbelief went out of him like the wind from a balloon and there was no place left for him to squirm to.

So we got it out of him.

It was like I'd figured, more or less. Odessa had had to lean on him hard, but Odessa had been good at that. Roscoe's ass was in a sling, Odessa had said, and since he, Odessa, was doing everything he could to help him, all he wanted was a favor in return. According to Roscoe, he'd only done Odessa a couple of such favors, though later on the "couple" became "several." All he'd done, in any case, was carry stuff back and forth between Paris and Amsterdam. He hadn't even known what he was carrying. Well, like he'd *known*, but he hadn't ever *looked*. What Odessa did was stuff his bag at the Paris end, and when they got home, Odessa took it from him and gave it back to him empty. The same thing in Amsterdam. Odessa's contact in Amsterdam was this blood called Wallace Edner. Odessa gave the money, or whatever it was, to Wallace, and Wallace came back with the stuff. And that was all there was to it.

"This Wallace Edner," I said to Valérie. "Wasn't he the one you were trying to find the other night?"

"Yes."

"Why'd you go looking for him?"

She looked at Roscoe, and Roscoe said: "Wallace is a good blood. I figured he could put us up at least."

"But he didn't?"

"No."

"Why not?"

"He said he couldn't. Said the word was out that ole Roscoe was bad news."

"Who'd put out the word?"

"I don' know. Mr. Lee maybe."

"Who's Mr. Lee?"

"I don' know. Some Dutch Chinaman. I used to hear him an' Odessa talkin' about Mr. Lee."

"Was he Wallace's boss?"

"I don' know. Maybe."

That made three I-don't-knows in a row, and two maybes.

"All right," I said, "let's take it back to the Paris end. Do you know who was bankrolling Odessa in Paris?"

"What do you mean, bankrollin'?"

"Just what I said. Odessa couldn't have had that kind of money, at least not in the beginning."

"He always carried a lot of cash."

"Not that kind of cash."

I was thinking of the figure Bobet had read out of his notebook. I was thinking of gang wars too, and the timing, and of something else Bobet had said: *The drug traffic in France isn't organized by any one person, Monsieur.*

"I don' know," repeated Roscoe, pulling at his hair. "Like I said, I was jus' doin' him a favor."

"So you said. But now, who else among the brothers was doing him favors?"

"Nobody, man. Leas' not at the start. It was too dangerous. Them that was in it was already doin' it for Delatour."

"You said not at the start. What about at the end?"

"I don' know, man. Odessa could put a lot of pressure on people."

"So some of the brothers ended up working for him too?"

"A couple, yeah."

"When did this happen?"

"I don' know exackly."

"But it was recent?"

"Yeah, recent."

I had, I thought, the makings of a fit.

"Was Atherton one of them?"

"Ath'ton? No, he was one of Delatour's."

That fit too.

There was no way, however, that I could get him to name names, not then, although next morning, when one of the Paris papers ran photos of every black American playing pro ball in France, he did better. Right then, though, it didn't matter that Odessa had lied to him, or that Odessa was dead, or that the rest of the brothers had stood by during the police investigation and let the murder accusation stand against him. It was black solidarity. Either it was black solidarity or else Roscoe Hadley, *né* Jimmie Cleever, was much naïver than I could credit him with.

He bounced back at dinner. All it took was a good meal, a bottle of wine, and an audience. Nico provided all three, and Roscoe, you could say, sang for more than his supper. He was king and jester rolled into one, talking about America, about Europe, about Parisians and Parisiennes, and his life and times on and off the hardwood, and all with that weird comical sophistication that made you forget he was a ghetto spade still on the underside of thirty. Long before we got to the coffee and cognac, he had Nico roaring with laughter and, strange to say, me as well. Only Valérie didn't join in. I caught her staring at me more than once across the dinner table. I tried to read her thoughts, without success. It was only after dinner, when we resumed our council of war, that she found her tongue again.

As for me, I had a theory going, and if, the way it worked out, you could say I tripped over my *modus operandi*, right then, in the comfort of Nico's living room, it looked worth pursuing. Sooner or later, I figured, we were going to have a choice to make; first off, though, I wanted to talk to Mr. Lee, the "Dutch Chinaman" Roscoe had mentioned. Furthermore, I wanted to do it without Roscoe. He was our trump card, and, as far as we knew, Nico's was what the cloak-and-dagger boys call a "safe house." Coming into Paris the night before, Valérie thought she might have been spotted. She'd ditched the car she'd rented and made the rendezvous with Billy Wheels on foot. But I was pretty sure we'd been clean all day, and in case we ran into trouble in Amsterdam, I wanted Roscoe out of it.

So far so good.

But then Valérie started to press me on what would happen after Mr. Lee.

"That depends," I said. "Sooner or later, we'll have to make a choice. It may be Roscoe will have to end up talking to the Law after all."

"Talkin' to what Law?" Roscoe said.

I summarized what Bobet and Frèrejean had said. I didn't like the idea of dealing with them any more than he did, but I thought there was at least a fair chance we could make the immunity stick.

Roscoe threw his head back and laughed.

"You must be out o' your mind, man. I'm not talkin' to no *Law!*"

"It could be either that or Delatour," I said.

"I don' see why it's got to be one or the other."

I started to answer, but Valérie cut me off.

"Then you'd better begin seeing it," she said sharply.

"There's nothin' to see, honey. They already 'xonerated me of Odessa's killin'. If I jus' tiptoe away, they'll forget the res'."

"Tiptoe away! You already ran from trouble once in your life! You swore you'd never do it again!"

"Who's talkin' about runnin'?" he said mildly. "I'm planning on stayin' right here awhile."

His tone drove her out of her chair.

"You're *what?*"

"Tha's right. While you was gone today, I worked it out with Nico. Says he can always use an extra hand on the milk farm. Says they got all kinds o' *sportin'* clubs in the towns aroun' here, kids 'n' men both. I could even do a little coachin' by 'n' by, teachin' ball.

Shoot, honey," he said, chuckling, "I always did want to try my hand milkin' *cows*...."

"For God's sake!" Valérie exploded at him. "They don't even milk cows by hand any more!"

"Well...," Roscoe began, but probably that was the last word he got in for a while.

"Cage!" Valérie said, holding him in her glare. "Leave us alone!"

I started to say something, but she cut me off too.

"Do what I say!" she said, whirling at me. "Please! Please leave us *alone!*"

Roscoe was staring at me, his big mouth ajar.

I went out then. I found Nico van den Luyken in his library, a small but well-proportioned room where another fire was blazing in the tiled hearth. We had one of those awkward conversations men sometimes get into. Clearly he wanted to talk about Valérie. I didn't. He seemed to assume we were both her ex-lovers, like privileged members of some exclusive club. Roscoe had beaten us out, it seemed, but that was all right with him. Anyway, Roscoe was really quite an extraordinary fellow, didn't I agree? Of course he was welcome to stay as long as he wanted to stay. Then Nico wanted to know if there was really nothing he could do. Valérie, he said, had told him very little, she hadn't wanted him to become involved more than necessary. That was all well and good, but if Roscoe was really in trouble, and quite serious trouble apparently...?

"There's one thing," I told him finally.

"What's that?"

"I don't think it will come to it, but if anything should happen to us, or any one of us, there's somebody you could call."

I dug out Frèrejean's number in Paris and gave it to him. This seemed to please him no end.

When I went back in, the living room was quiet as a morgue. Roscoe had his head down and palmed between his big hands, like he was trying to shut out sound. Valérie was slumped in a chair, small-faced and tense. Clearly she hadn't gotten what she wanted, and from my own experience I could guess this came as quite a shock to her.

And that was that.

I spent the night under an eiderdown, in a guest room big enough for a platoon of lovers. I spent it alone, though.

As far as I know, we all did.

=12=

"Who's Looie the Luke?" I said.

"Leduc," Valérie answered. "Jean-Louis Leduc."

We were in the Beetle, heading north, alone. The rain had stopped during the night, but there was a stiff wind blowing off the North Sea and it was whipping clouds in bunches over the flat, water-streaked land. The Beetle was doing better in the wind than we were. Neither of us had mentioned the night before, but it was there, between us, and conversation had become a sometime thing.

The name—"Looie the Luke"—had come up at breakfast. It had been Roscoe's contribution. "Looie the Luke," he'd said, "or Flooie the Fluke, something like that. Odessa mentioned him."

In fact, he remembered, Odessa had gone looking for him once when they'd come back to Paris.

Jean-Louis Leduc. Bobby H., it seemed to me, had mentioned him too, and so did the papers we saw at breakfast. According to the papers, Leduc was the registered owner of the Place Clichy brasserie that had been shot up. But not one of the wounded, or dead.

That fit too.

"What do you know about him?" I asked Valérie in the Beetle.

"Not much. They call him Loulou in the underworld. He's old, an old-style *caïd*. He was in the Resistance, or so they say."

"What's a *caïd*?"

"A boss. It's an Arab word."

"The same as 'big bonnet'?"

"In a way."

"Is Delatour one too?"

"No. There's a difference."

"He'd like to be, though, wouldn't he?"

"Yes."

"And Leduc would be somebody he'd have to muscle out of his way?"

"Yes."

"Did you know he was dealing in dope too? Leduc, I mean?"

"No."

It stood to reason, though. *The drug traffic in France isn't organized by any one person,* and Dédé Delatour had come up with a pretty clever scheme to push his way in. Only Leduc had subverted part of the scheme, by bankrolling Odessa Grimes himself. So Delatour had had to punish Leduc, by way of Odessa's murder, and Leduc had retaliated, I figured, by giving Atherton to the Law. ("We have our sources of information," Bobet had said.) Whereupon Delatour had upped the ante drastically, as befit a *caïd*-on-the-make, and now there was Leduc blood splattered all over the streets of Paris.

So far, it appeared, all the escalation had been on Delatour's part. But unless I missed my guess, or the Law stepped in first to stop it, the next move was up to Loulou Leduc.

I've referred to my *modus operandi.* What I had in mind, broadly speaking, was the gathering and suppression of information, a technique I used to be pretty good at in my California days. The way it looked to me on the rainy road to Amsterdam, Roscoe had two things going for him: one was his body; the other was what he knew, or could be made to appear to know. I was hopeful of using the second to save the first. In the meantime, though, until such time as we could make a deal, it seemed like a good idea to keep the body at Nico van den Luyken's.

Roscoe thought so too.

Valérie may have thought otherwise, but it was hard to know what she thought that morning, other than that she was down on the male sex in general. Not that you'd have known it to look at her. She was wearing a skirt-and-sweater combination in a dusty-rose jersey wool, with a long tunic to match, dark leather boots, and white trenchcoat, and her hair glistened blond in the gray air. I thought again about Nico's resources and complimented her on the fit of her clothes.

"They ought to fit," she said.

"What do you mean?"

"They're mine," she said, her jaw jutting firmly forward.

The drawer opened, the drawer closed.

End of conversation.

We came into Amsterdam off the Hague-Rotterdam autoroute and wound our way across the canals into that old and seedy part of town around the Zeedijk which is fobbed off to the tourists as the Sailors' Quarter. It's pretty colorful of a summer night, when the red-lit whores display their offerings in ground-floor windows, and maybe you could even find a bona-fide seaman among the nocturnal flotsam of tourists and international youth, but on a gray morning in late fall, with the rain falling again in wind-driven gusts and the cobbles awash in sodden debris, well, you'd settle for Wallace Edner too.

Wallace Edner had the build and the stoop of Roscoe, but his playing days were clearly over. Lines as deep as gullies surrounded his mouth, and the blood that speckled his eyeballs looked like it had come to stay. We found him in the same saloon where Roscoe and Valérie had tracked him down. It was a mock-Western joint where the dust gathered like tumbleweed under the bar rail and the daylight had to fight its way in. At the back end of the bar, Wallace Edner was just emptying a shot of whiskey into his mid-morning schooner of beer.

"Good morning, Wallace," I said.

He looked at me, gloomy and red-eyed, then at Valérie. If he recognized her right off, though, he didn't show it.

"We want to see Mr. Lee," I said.

"Mr. Lee?" he said. "Now, which Mr. Lee would that be?"

He took an experimental sip from the glass mug. He swallowed, grimacing a little, then, when that stayed down, helped himself to a larger slug.

"I didn't know there was more than one," I said.

"There's lots of Mr. Lees," he answered.

I took out a hundred-florin note, worth about forty U.S. dollars, and laid it on the bar. I ordered another round for Wallace Edner, and beers for Valérie and me. The beer was better than passable, but Wallace Edner pushed his aside and simply added the second shot of whiskey to the schooner in front of him.

"That narrows it down some," he said, grinning. His mouth had a lot of metal in it, with gaps between. "What you say your name was?"

"I didn't," I said. "I don't know that it would mean anything to Mr. Lee. Just tell him I'm a friend of Loulou's."

"Loulou's?"

"Leduc," I said. "Monsieur Leduc, from Paris."

"I don' know about any Ledook."

"That's all right. I think Mr. Lee will."

"If we're talkin' about the same Mr. Lee."

"I think we are," I said. "The one I'm talking about is in import-export."

He liked that. He repeated it, "import-export," and the wrinkles carved his face and he laughed a gap-toothed laugh. Then he took another hefty swallow. Then he said:

"What's your shit, Mister?"

"What do you mean?"

He glanced at me, frowning a little.

"What you buyin'? You don' got to see the big man in order to buy."

"I didn't say I was buying. I said I wanted to talk to Mr. Lee."

He liked that less. He said his Mr. Lee was a busy man, he didn't have the time just to talk. In fact, he liked it so little that he wasn't sure after all that his Mr. Lee and mine were the same Mr. Lee.

I caught his message. It cost me another round of drinks and a new hundred-florin note to make him like it better.

He went out into the street finally, ducking his head at the doorway. He was gone awhile. When he came back, we'd moved to a table, and he blinked his eyes in the dimness, swiveling his head till he found us.

"You got wheels?" he said, standing over me. He rested the fingertips of one hand on the tabletop.

"Yes. Why?"

"It's wet outside. A man don' like to get wet. I tell you what. You bring yo' wheels back about three, a bit befo', I'll take you to see Mr. Lee."

I glanced at my watch.

—131—

"Three's a long way off," I said.

"I tole you," said Wallace Edner. "He's a *busy* man."

We had time to kill. We killed some of it riding around the city in the Beetle, and more of it on foot. We changed some more of Bobby H.'s francs in a bank. We went to a shop I'd been to before on the Leidsestraat. I bought a pipe there and an umbrella across the street. For lunch we went to a famous downtown beef joint which is something like a hundred years old and five million steaks old. And all this time, from the moment we left the Zeedijk saloon, the tails stayed with us. There were two of them in a car, at least one on foot when we were walking, and they made no great effort at concealment. I didn't like it particularly, but I wasn't surprised. I mean, even in a city as wide open as Amsterdam, you didn't just walk in and ask to see a leading dope merchant without arousing attention.

We went back to the bar a little before three. Wallace was wrapped around another boilermaker, and, to judge from the boozy effluvium he gave off, he hadn't even taken time out for lunch.

I told him we were ready.

He shook his head mournfully at me.

I'd gotten it wrong, he said. *We* may have been ready, but *I* was the only one he was taking.

"Roscoe's girl stays here," he said.

The magic name had come up at last.

Between the name and the way Wallace shrugged when I started to argue with him, my stomach jumped like a frog. It was one of those what-have-I-gotten-us-into feelings, like when you're up on the high bar and they're taking the net away. But Wallace had set up the appointment for me only, and that was the way it was going to be.

Else, he said, nobody was going nowhere.

I looked at Valérie.

"It's O.K.," she said, smiling at me. "I'll wait for you here. The ones who've been following us all day will take care of me."

I hadn't realized she'd spotted them too.

The smile may have cost her an effort, but it was a nice smile. I managed to return it.

The Prinsengracht is the last of Amsterdam's inner ring of canals. A few hundred years back, in the heyday of the Dutch Empire, it had been a beehive of trade, but nowadays the narrow brick merchants' homes are mostly banks and galleries and the boats on the tree-lined waterway are carting tourists. It was about the last place, in sum, you'd have expected to find someone in Mr. Lee's line, although there was a nice irony in the idea that the old function of import-export had returned to the canals. Twentieth-century style.

The front was a travel agency specializing in the Oriental, and probably if you'd walked in off the street you actually could have bought a round trip to Rangoon. As for me, I was given the five-star reception. Two over-sized Easterners met me at the front door, a handsome brass-knockered affair, and led me up a narrow wood staircase with polished steps and polished mahogany banisters and polished brass knobs. The escorts were pretty polished too, and so was the way they frisked me before they ushered me into Mr. Lee's office.

This was a large room, with scrollwork on the ceiling, a Persian rug on the floor, a wood fire burning in the grate, and a view out over the canal. It had a massive wood desk which shone like a mirror, and several captain's chairs grouped around the desk for visitors. The desktop was completely bare, except for Mr. Lee's hands.

It was hard to imagine him in a pigtail. From his clothes to his accent, he was pure Savile Row. He had on a dark-blue suit, a thin-striped blue-and-white shirt with white collar, a figured silk tie held in place by a pearl-topped pin. His cufflinks had pearls too, and the silk tips of a handkerchief protruded from his breast pocket. But what struck me even more was his age. Or lack of it. Even allowing for the proverbial inscrutability of his race, he couldn't have been more than in his mid-thirties, and maybe a good deal younger. There wasn't a line on his broad face. His eyes were dark and the whites clear, his hair jet black and straight. He had too a disconcertingly calm air, the kind you'd associate more readily with yellow-bearded ancients who've had their brains softened by the poppy. It was like when the world blew up around him, young Mr. Lee would still be sitting there, his hands folded on the gleaming desktop, waiting for business.

"Good afternoon, Mr. Cage," he said without moving. "Sit down."

I wondered briefly where he'd gotten my name. He answered it for me, in his way.

"You've come up in several connections recently," he said. "I thought we should meet."

"I did too," I said. I sat down across from him. "In that case," I went on, "we can dispense with the niceties. I didn't come here to buy. I imagine you know that. I've got something to sell."

I waited for him to ask me what. He didn't. Evidently the question was superfluous.

"Roscoe Hadley's silence," I said.

He answered without moving a muscle: "What makes you think I would be interested in that?"

"I'm not sure you would be, directly. But some of your customers are."

"I do business with a great many people," he replied.

"Like Didier Delatour? Like Jean-Louis Leduc?"

"Names," he said blandly. "In fact, what my customers do and don't do outside our transactions is not my concern."

"Isn't it? Well, in case you haven't heard, your French market's in the process of going up in smoke. From what I hear, the streets of Paris are being turned into a battlefield. Is that no concern of yours?"

The shrug, if there was one, was limited to his voice.

"France is a turbulent country, Mr. Cage. It has been before, it will be again."

Sure, I'd come there on a long shot. There was nothing that obliged him to deal with me, and I knew it. But around about then his see-no-evil hear-no-evil style started to get under my skin.

"Come on, Mr. Lee," I said, "you're a businessman, your business depends on stable markets like any other. It's not my lookout, but if you ask me, you've let them do a pretty half-assed job of organizing France. Maybe you think now that you can wait till the smoke clears and trade with whoever survives, but you're running a hell of a risk that nobody's going to survive. Because, more than likely, the ones who aren't dead are going to end up in jail."

"That might be true," he said imperturbably, "or false. But I don't see what it has to do with what you have to sell."

"Oh, no?" I answered. "I'd've thought you'd be better informed. In case nobody's told you, Roscoe Hadley has been in the thick of it.

He knows where the bodies are buried, the live ones as well as the dead. He knows who's been running dope for Delatour, for Leduc as well. He's got the network in his head, Mr. Lee, the basketball network but not just the basketball network, names and addresses, and not only in France. He's even got yours, Mr. Lee. I'm here because he told me where to go. If you ask me, he's got a lot to do with it, a whole lot, and if he spills it to the wrong people, he could put the dope trade in Europe back into the Dark Ages."

Whatever was true in this, or false, it visibly failed to move him.

"All right," I said angrily, pushing back my chair. "If you're not interested, I'm going to keep looking till I find somebody who is. Even if it means the Law."

I stood up and headed for the door. I meant what I'd said. Whether Roscoe liked it or not. Whether *I* liked it or not.

Sometimes you've got to take what you can get.

"One moment, please," his voice said behind me.

I turned.

The only change in his posture was that he'd unfolded his hands. They lay flat on the desk now, immobile, immaculate.

"It is true that I'm not interested," he said, following me with his eyes. "But in the event that I might know someone who is, what precisely is your propostion?"

"I told you," I said, still standing. "I'm ready to sell Hadley's silence. To the highest bidder."

"What do you want in exchange?"

"Immunity and protection," I said. "For Hadley, for Valérie Merchadier, for myself."

"Immunity and protection from what?"

"From the police, for one. And from your customers."

"How do you propose that these things be guaranteed?"

"That's for you to work out—or your customers. But it shouldn't be too difficult. By way of an example, let me give you one element that might be part of the package. Supposing that all Hadley wants is to go on playing basketball in France. As long as he can do that and stay alive and well, then he's happy, then everybody's happy. Now let's suppose, in addition, that he were to make out a deposition, a detailed one, concerning the drug trade, with all the names and addresses spelled out. Let's suppose, even, that such a deposition already exists, in several copies, each one signed and witnessed and notarized, and that these copies are already in safe hands, with instructions, should anything happen to him, on where they are to be sent. Do you follow me?"

It would be nice to say that he narrowed his eyes, bad-guy style. He didn't, though. He simply looked at me, palms flat, inscrutable.

"While we're in the realm of hypothesis," he said finally, "let me suggest another one."

"Please do," I said.

"Suppose that someone were interested in buying, not Hadley's silence, but Hadley himself? With the same kind of immunity and protection you have talked about, for you and the woman? As well as a cash payment, the sum of which would be a subject for negotiation?"

It was my turn, then, to keep my lids up. And the grin off my face.

We studied each other. He was waiting for me to answer. I let him wait.

"How much, Mr. Cage?" asked the Chinaman.

I shook my head.

"No sale," I said. "Hadley himself is not for sale."

He seemed to be considering that for a minute. Again he didn't move, unless it was with a part of his body outside my line of vision.

"You are a short-sighted man," he said.

"A dumb one, you mean," an American voice blurted out behind me.

It all happened so fast I can't give the sequence of events. Maybe the Chinaman had a signal button under his feet, maybe he did it by thought waves. I hadn't so much as heard the door open behind me.

I recognized the voice as I turned, even before I saw him. By then, though, it was already too late.

There was a desk between me and the Chinaman, but nothing but space between me and Johnny Vee and his muscle. Space and a blunt-nosed submachine gun.

We stared at each other.

"Hello, Johnny Boy," I said. "You're a long way from Malibu, aren't you?"

"Yeah," he said. "And it always seems to be you that brings me over to this shithole."

The reference was to events that I've described elsewhere. I won't go into them now. I've described him before too. He was good-looking, I guess, in a flashy, guinea way. He'd been born into the California mob and had risen steadily through the ranks, but more, I'd always thought, out of nepotism than by merit.

I'd known him a long time. Suffice it that he'd never made the top ten on my Favorite Gangster list.

"Lee and Vee," I said, looking from one to the other, "a Chinese laundry with Italian pressers. But I must say," focusing on the Chinaman, "I'd've thought you'd be more discriminating in the people you got involved with."

Mr. Lee didn't answer.

"You slant-eyed son of a bitch," I said. "You were playing with me the whole time, weren't you?"

His only reaction was that he stood up.

The script called for a little rough stuff then, and Johnny Vee was never one to disappoint his biographers. It was mostly for show, though. A travel agency on the Prinsengracht, after all, is no place for blood and guns. Then Johnny's muscle had me out on the canal bank, and the last thing I saw before they shoved me into the car and put on the blindfold was that Wallace Edner had disappeared, and the Beetle with him.

There were five of us in the car. The one with the submachine gun and Johnny himself surrounded me in the back seat. The two up front were slant-eyed talent, courtesy of Mr. Lee. It was a combined operation all right, but what I didn't realize then was that we were only the rear guard of an army.

=13=

In between then and nightfall, Johnny Vee had time for some funning with me.

"You're really stooping low, punk," he said. "When you pimped for the rich, you were still a punk, but at least you had some class then. Now you're down to coons and their French cunts. That's stooping pretty low, if you ask me."

"Nobody asked you," I said.

I was sitting in a chair, backed against the wall of a room which was next to a sort of air shaft. I figured we were still in Amsterdam. I was tied to the chair, something that was getting to be a habit with me, with my legs straddled outside the chair legs. They'd taken the blindfold off. Johnny Vee was standing in front of me, one foot propped on the seat of the chair. The tip of his shoe was about three inches from my scrotum, and the rest of him was leaning over me, rocking slightly. I got a good whiff of brilliantine.

"The French cunt's not bad, honh?" he said. "A little skinny in the ass, the French cunts always are, but she handles good. From what I hear, she ought to, isn't that so, punk?"

I didn't answer, not even when he rocked closer with the tip of his shoe.

"Where's Cleever, punk?" he said. "Or what is it he calls himself now? Hadley? Where's Hadley, punk?"

I didn't answer that either.

"Maybe the cunt'll tell us, whadda you think? D'you want me to bring her in here and fuck her in front of you?"

His face was close to mine, and grinning.

"Go ahead," I said. "I always wondered if you could get it up."

The grin vanished and his head jerked back. At the same time his foot slammed forward, catching me full in the balls. My chair smacked against the wall. A shock of pain shot toward my brain, but then it splintered, north, east, south, west. My eyes watered and a spurt of vomit surged into my throat. For some reason, I fought it down.

Johnny Vee was standing back. He was laughing his guinea head off.

"D'you think we needed *you* to find him?" he shouted. "You're dumb, punk! I always knew you were dumb, but they must've thrown away the mold after you! Whaddid you think? That Cleever and the cunt could walk into a town like this and out again? You're in against the *pros* this time, punk! And you're nothin' but a fuckin' *amatoor!* We had Cleever and the cunt fingered two days ago!"

My eyes started to clear. I salivated, tasted vomit, swallowed.

"Who's we?" I said weakly.

"Me and the Dutch, dumbie. The careful, punctual Dutch."

"What took you so long?"

"We were waiting on *you*, dumbie, whadda you think?"

He made a big grinning thing out of what he was going to do with me. He said he'd told Delatour to cut my balls off. He said he'd told the Chink to use them for fish bait and dump the rest of me into the canal. He had similar projects in mind for Roscoe and Valérie. All in all, he was very big on genitals, was Johnny Vee.

After a while, though, he must have run short of ideas. He went out, leaving me in the keep of his muscle. Little by little the pain localized in my scrotum, and while it throbbed, I tried to sort out what had happened.

Any way you sliced it, it looked like a disaster for the home team. If Roscoe or Valérie was still on the loose, that kick in the balls would only have been for openers. I wondered, though, what they'd done about Nico. You didn't mess around with a van den Luyken in Holland and expect the Law to look the other way. Maybe Johnny Vee would have tried if he was acting on his own, but clearly he wasn't. On the other hand, I could only speculate as to what he was doing there, six thousand miles from home, and it didn't enter my head then that he'd changed sides.

They waited till dark, I think, to move me. If I'm vague about the timing, it's because of the coffee. At some point, there was a lot of stirring around in the hall outside, and somebody came in and asked me if I wanted a cup. I'd have liked whiskey better, but coffee would do. The guy who'd been handling the submachine gun on the Prinsengracht brought it in and fed it to me. Or tried to. I took a sip, gagged, and spat it out. In the end it took two of them to get it down, one forcing my jaws open while the other poured. I gagged and sputtered and hollered and spat, but some of it got past my gullet, enough anyway so that later, when they put the blindfold back on and cut me loose, I was already wobbling and disoriented.

A Chinese recipe, I presume.

They had to take off the blindfold for border crossings and toll booths. It didn't make any difference. I was sandwiched in the back seat between two of my fellow countrymen, and when we came through a checkpoint, one of them shoved a gun into me, high on the ribs under the armpit. He needn't have bothered with that either. Whatever had been in the coffee, it had set up a barrier between my brain and my voice, and my tongue felt like a slab of concrete laid between my teeth. When I dozed off, I thought I was still awake; when I was awake, it was like I was dreaming. The car, I remember, was a Citroën, a CX in the 2000 series. I remember seeing the big single windshield wiper slicking back and forth across the oncoming headlights, back and forth, and some synapse of insight a long way off told me it must be raining. I remember stopping at the frontier—probably it was the one between Mons and Valenciennes—and the guard taking the passports from the driver and crouching to look into the car, and it was like I was looking back at him from inside two long lasers of light, and my mind was shouting NICO! TELEPHONE! NICO! so fucking loud it set off shivers of nausea in the light tunnels. But if Nico was still alive, then he hadn't called, or if he'd called, then they hadn't answered at the other end, or if they'd answered at the other end, then Frèrejean had sent out the word by ordinary mail and the border posts wouldn't get the message till the Wells Fargo express made the next run north from Paris. Because all the guard did at the end of the light tunnels was count eyeballs and divide by two and compare and contrast to the number of passports he held in his hand, which he handed back to the driver, who handed them to his partner, and off we rolled out of the tunnels into the blackness of the République Française. Then I must have dropped off again, because what I saw was signs, one after the other, sweeping in over my head with the regularity of telephone poles when you're looking out a train window, and the signs said PARIS PARIS PARIS, white block letters on a dark field, and there were white stub arrows under the words sweeping me through, one after the other.

 I've said we were only the rear guard of an army. There must have been at least three such cars rolling south that night toward Paris, but as it turned out, the main forces were already waiting for us. Somewhere between the Survilliers toll booth and the end of the autoroute, they tied my hands behind my back and put the blindfold on again. The drug seemed to be wearing off. I could tell that when we hit the Porte de la Chapelle interchange we turned west onto the Périphérique, and we went on for a few exits—the Porte de St. Ouen maybe, or Clichy—before entering the city itself. But then the disorientation took over again—cobbles, smooth pavement, more cobbles—and when we stopped, all I knew about the end of the line was that it was somewhere near the northern rim of Paris.

I shivered briefly in cold air. Then we were inside a building and going up in an elevator. The elevator was one of those old-fashioned jobs, built for families of midgets. Three of us, I think, wedged in together. I heard the gate clank shut. Then we went up slowly, maybe to the top. When we got out on the landing, a door opened immediately. I was shoved inside. I could hear voices, several of them. They were talking in French.

We went down what was probably a hallway, a very long one with hooks in it. In front of me, somebody said, *"On va le mettre ici, celui-là,"* which meant, "We'll put this one here." Then I was pushed forward until something hit me hard, about mid-thigh. I heard a door shut behind me, a lock turn.

They left it to me to get the blindfold off. This meant untying my hands first. This I did eventually, with the help of a friendly faucet. What I'd bumped into was a bathroom sink. The bathroom, to judge, had also been designed for midgets, and it was unused. I found a light switch, but it turned out there was no bulb in the ceiling socket. With the coming of false dawn, a faint light penetrated the half-window in the back wall. By then, though, feeling my way around, I'd already identified the furnishings: a sink, a sit-up bathtub, a bidet under the window, a waist-high wall cupboard.

The cupboard was empty. There were no plugs in the drains. Only cold water ran through the taps.

I spent quite a while splashing my face with the cold water. This had a weirdly tonic effect. It set all sorts of projects flushing through my brain.

I was going to make a rope out of my clothes and go out the window. If I couldn't get to the ground, I could at least get to a window on the floor below. If I couldn't get to a window on the floor below, at least I'd attract some attention.

This necessitated getting the window open first. Standing on the bidet in order to reach it, I found out that the window was painted shut, not just the lock but all the seams.

This didn't seem much of an obstacle. If worse came to worst, I could knock the glass out with my fist. To do it quietly enough, all I had to do was wrap my shirt around my fist.

This necessitated getting my shirt off.

If the window was too small for me to get my body through, I could always plug up the drain of the sink with my shirt and let the water overflow till it seeped through the floorboards. Failing that, I could write a message on a piece of my shirt and send it out through the plumbing.

If I could find a pen.

If I couldn't, I could always use blood.

Most of these ventures required my getting my shirt off. I remember trying. The next thing I remember, it was still on and I was waking up on the floor. My body was hugging the sit-in bathtub. I had a blinding headache and the nausea was pulsing through me in monotonous waves.

I threw up in the sink and felt a little better. It was light outside. Standing on the bidet, I realized it was just as well I hadn't gotten my shirt off. We were high up, very high for that part of Paris. Below me were the corners of some rooftops. They looked like quite a jump away. Beyond them, the buildings sloped up quickly, and humped up against the gray sky above them I saw the white rear façade of Sacré Coeur.

This put me somewhere behind the Butte Montmartre, in the back of the 18th Arrondissement.

I sat down on the little step in the bathtub. My watch said ten after two. I wound it some. It still said ten after two.

A little later they came for me.

14

If the bathroom had been designed for midgets, it was the only such part of the apartment. Probably my wing was for servants. The other rooms I glimpsed from the hallway were big and empty, and not only empty but bare, uninhabited.

All, that is, except for two.

One escort went up the hallway in front of me, another behind. They had a kind of hoody elegance about them, like they were going to a wedding or a funeral. I didn't recognize either one.

We stopped outside a pair of double doors. They were closed, but I could hear voices inside. The front escort knocked. Somebody opened from the inside, and I was ushered in.

In the old days they'd have called this the salon. Nowadays, in the real-estate ads, it would go as a double living room, which meant two large rooms separated by an archway. Running their length on the far side was a series of glass-paned double doors that gave onto a terrace, with a view of the Butte Montmartre. The terrace doors were closed when I came in, but I saw a couple of muscle taking the air outside.

The room to my left was empty except for a long buffet table covered with white napery. There were cups and saucers stacked on it, and silver pots on trays, and glasses of various sizes backed by an assortment of bottles. From time to time, while I was there, people went in and helped themselves. Except for those who rated service.

It was strictly a suit-and-tie affair. Those who rated service—some eight men in all—sat in a semi-circle, each with a small end-table next to him. Johnny Vee, the new boy in town, was the youngest of the semi-circle by a pretty fair margin. He'd changed sides, all right. He was also the most subdued Johnny Vee I'd ever seen, though this may have been due to language as well as to the generation gap. A ninth man sat close to him and a little behind, and served as interpreter. Behind them circulated a motley of muscle, including a couple of Americans, but except for an unlikely bulge here and there, I saw no signs of artillery.

The only woman on hand was Valérie Merchadier. They had her in the middle of a row of three chairs, facing the semi-circle and the terrace beyond it. Roscoe slouched in the far chair. Neither of them was bound, but each had a guard standing close behind.

Valérie's eyes followed me in. A little bedraggled, but physically intact. Roscoe, though, was another story. His body had gone slack, limp, like somebody'd taken him by the scruff, like a rag doll, and shaken too long. His gaze was vague, unseeing, and a bad-looking gash ran west from the bridge of his nose across the cheekbone. Conceivably he'd put up a struggle when they took him. More likely, I thought, Johnny Vee had been dividing his leisure time.

The empty chair was for me. I sat down, blinking in the harsh sunlight that came from the terrace and trying to identify the expression I'd seen in Valérie's eyes.

I hadn't seen it before. It wasn't surprise. It took me a little while to realize, simply, that she was scared stiff.

With reason, I'll add. The discussion was in French, and to judge from the smoke that layered up toward the ceiling, it had been going on for some time. In form, it could have been any business conference anywhere. What was disconcerting, though, was that it went on even after I'd been brought in. Like I wasn't there. Whereas, given what they were talking about, I kind of doubted they intended to make it public.

A spare, bony Frenchman with tired and well-bagged eyes was doing most of the talking. I took him for the chairman of the board. It was only later that I realized that he was just fronting for the man to his right. His name, I found out subsequently, was Verucci, and he handled the language like an orator. He also had a police record as long as your arm.

When I got there, Verucci was in the midst of some sort of summing up. It was agreed, he said in substance, that order should be restored, in Paris and elsewhere, by the quickest possible means. The plan proposed to the council was accepted; it would be executed without delay. The offer of collaboration from their new American colleague (here he turned and nodded briefly toward Johnny Vee) was also accepted. Once the problem of the competition was resolved and order restored, the new marketing arrangements would go into effect immediately. Insofar as sports were concerned—*le sport*, as he put it—and particularly those sectors which employed foreign athletes, namely *le basket*, this would now come under the supervision of their American colleague, through the interposed parties as agreed.

What I took this to mean, allowing for the flourishes of Verucci's tongue and the hazards of translation, was (1) that Dédé Delatour was to be erased, quickly and violently; (2) that the dope traffic in France was to be consolidated under mob control; and (3) that the new, if hidden, czar of French basketball was that eminent California sportsman, Johnny Vee.

He was still climbing, was Johnny Vee. He'd just gone multinational.

The vote went around the semi-circle. Some of them grunted; some of them just nodded. Nobody dissented.

There was a stirring then, like it was coffee-break time.

"*Bien*," said the man to Verucci's right, speaking for the first time. "*Et ces trois-là?*"

He was referring to the three of us.

The stirring stopped.

I could see what Valérie had meant when she'd called him a *caïd*. It was a question of authority. He was bulky and old, with a massive head in which presided two deep-sunk dark eyes. He had a ruined trunk of a nose with a mole on it, and white hair growing out of the mole, and thinning wisps of white hair on his skull.

Down among the Allah-worshipers, a *caïd* is at once the judge and the chief of police. In other words, when Leduc spoke, the stirring stopped.

Verucci introduced us then, succinctly.

The black was an American. He played basketball professionally. He'd worked for the other black, the one who was dead.

The woman was his concubine. She was also the daughter of the lawyer Merchadier.

As for me, I was a small-time American detective, operating in Paris.

Not much of an epitaph.

We'd been the cause of considerable embarrassment to the council, Verucci went on. We had also embarrassed their colleague in Amsterdam. We had also, in the past, embarrassed Monsieur Vee.

At this point, Leduc pulled Verucci's sleeve. The spokesman

leaned down and Leduc said something in his ear.

"Yes," Verucci said, straightening up. "Accessorily, there is the question of depositions. The detective Cage told our colleague in Amsterdam that the black had prepared depositions describing our activities in certain areas. Should anything happen to him, Cage threatened, these documents would be given wide publicity. According to the black and his concubine, however, no such documents exist. They..."

"I'm sorry, Cage!" Valérie blurted out. "I didn't know you'd..."

"*Shut up! Speak when spoken to!*"

Leduc's voice cracked out like thunder. He half rose out of his chair.

What Valérie said to him then, hissing the words, brought him the rest of the way to his feet.

Valérie's guard seized her from behind, tipping her chair back, and when I started forward, my windpipe ran into a forearm of steel. I went back too, in mid-air, while Leduc crossed the intervening space.

He moved with surprising quickness. Valérie kicked out at him, but he knocked her leg aside and, stepping inside it, reached down and grabbed a handful of breast through her sweater.

I saw him wrench. I heard her gasp, cry out.

He let her go. His chest was heaving. He stepped back and turned to me.

"You lied to the Chinaman," he said. "The documents don't exist."

It came out a statement, not a question, and the black glare followed from deep inside his skull.

I couldn't speak. At a nod from Leduc, the forearm relaxed its pressure. I felt the floor under my feet again.

"It doesn't matter what I say now, does it?" I answered. "Maybe they exist, maybe they don't, but how will you be able to tell whether I'm telling the truth? There's only one sure way for you to find out, Loulou."

The forearm struck again. I guess the muscle didn't like hearing the boss addressed by his nickname. But Leduc waved him off.

"You like to live dangerously," he said to me. "But either way, the black doesn't know enough about our operations to hurt us."

"No? Well, maybe he does, maybe he doesn't, but that would be for the Law to judge, wouldn't it? And the press? It would depend, for one thing, on how much Grimes might have told him, if you see what I mean. But that's not the point, not at all. Don't you see?"

I leaned forward as far as I could get and raised my voice.

"You just decided—*all* of you—to get Delatour. A unanimous vote, isn't that right? And maybe you can, *probably* you can, even though Delatour's no shrinking violet. But a lot of people are likely to get killed in the bargain, and who's to say it'll end there? I never knew anybody worth a damn in your business who took needless risks, and if you ask me, you're about to take a monumental one. Whereas if you let Hadley do it for you, let him spill what he knows to the Law, they'd have enough on Delatour and his gang to put them on ice till we're all dead and buried."

I had more to say than that and they let me say it all. I did it big. It was like I was on the free-throw line with the score tied and time run out. The crowd was on its feet and Roscoe on the bench. It was up to Cage now. Now or never.

Only somehow I still held the ball in my hands. The longer I held it, the heavier it got. And when I was done talking, it was like a sphere full of mud.

The thing was: I'd been banking on being able to feed Delatour to the wolves and on the wolves being satisfied. Let Roscoe sing to the Law, let the Law hang Delatour, let Leduc's operations continue as before. All of which would depend, obviously, on how much influence Leduc still had going for him.

But when I'd finished, Leduc spoke out, cold-eyed.

"You're too late with that now," he said.

And that was all he said. And then he snapped his fists apart, like he was breaking a stick of wood.

What chilled my blood even more doesn't come through in English. French, like a lot of other languages, has two ways of saying "you." One is *tu*, the other is *vous*. *Vous* is what you say in normal conversation. *Tu* is what the grammar books call the "intimate" form. That means you can use it in bed. But *tu* is also used in other I'm-on-top, you're-on-the-bottom situations. French parents, for instance, use it in talking to their children, and French masters to their servants, and the French generally to Ayrabs and blackamoors. And executioners, presumably, in that tender moment near the end when they ask their victim if they've any last requests.

What I'm getting at is that Loulou Leduc had used it on me.

15

Maybe it's the instinct for self-preservation, maybe the proverbial optimism of Americans, but I've always had trouble believing somebody would actually order up my extinction. Sure I've been in combat, and you could argue that the poor slobs shooting at me had been ordered to by some general in a war room with his finger on the map. But the general in question had slant eyes and yellow skin, and his target wasn't me, Cage, but anything that was white and moved. I've also been in man-on-man situations a few times where death by violence, mine or his, was a logical possibility, and once or twice I was plain lucky. But that somebody in power, somebody who'd laid eyes on me and talked to me in human conversation, could actually point the finger, saying, "That one, kill him," and mean me, Cage, B. F., and not the guy down the street...

No. No way.

I came as close, though, to believing it that day as I ever have. We'd been a source of embarrassment to them. Alive, we'd continue to be. It didn't matter in this sense how much we knew, or how little. Dédé Delatour was to be eliminated, quickly and violently, bullets were going to fly and blood spill, and three more corpses in the body count wouldn't make a hell of a lot of difference.

In other words, the source of embarrassment would be removed. And when it comes to the mob, be it U.S. or French or Pakistani, there's only one way they go about such things.

After my exchange with Leduc, Verucci began to summarize the solutions that had been proposed in our regard. The one suggested by their American colleague merited particular attention, in his opinion. There were several other possibilities, but...

At this point, though, Leduc cut him off.

"Get them out of here," he ordered peremptorily.

I expected us to be separated again. Then, when they stuck us in the empty room at the other end of the hallway, with armed muscle between us and the door, I thought we'd be called back to hear the verdict. But it didn't happen like that. Instead, we sat there on the bare floorboards, waiting, listening.

While Valérie hugged her knees.

And our star witness kept his back to the wall, his feet splayed out in front of him.

And the muscle sat on straight chairs.

And I tried to guess their American colleague's solution.

After a while, we swapped stories.

Valérie's, it turned out, was little different from mine. They'd taken her as soon as Wallace Edner and I left the Zeedijk bar, two men with guns and a car waiting outside. She'd been blindfolded too, part of the time, and Johnny Vee had worked her over personally in ways she didn't want to talk about. It damn near broke her up that she hadn't caught on about the depositions. What she'd said, on the spot, was that she didn't know anything about them. Later on, she'd been transported to Paris the same way I had, coffee included. She thought it had still been light outside when they left Amsterdam, but she wasn't sure.

Roscoe had been lifted right out of Nico's house, in broad daylight. The trouble was that there, on the floor of that empty room, he went into another non-remembering phase. It was like the stuffing had been knocked out of him and something else besides, and what was left you could only call a reversion to the nigger mentality: the idea that the honkies had fucked him over again, present company included, and not for the first time, and probably not for the last. About all we got out of him was that, either by design or accident, they'd grabbed him when Nico wasn't there. They'd come fast too, like it had been planned. That, and that the one who'd done the job on him later was also Johnny Vee.

The California sportsman, it seemed, had had a full day.

There was a ray of hope, though, in what Roscoe said, for people looking for rays of hope. That was Nico. I was pretty sure he'd have made the call to Frèrejean, given the chance. But I had no way of knowing if he'd been given the chance.

Time passed.

We heard people coming and going in the apartment.

At some point in the afternoon, the muscle guarding us were replaced by other muscle.

Meanwhile, we were still alive. I wasn't sure why, but by and by I began to get used to the idea, and the more I got used to it, the better I liked it. Call that self-preservation if you want to, but it started the adrenalin flowing again.

Sometimes, like I said, you take what you can get.

It was late afternoon when they took us down in the elevator, one by one.

We all met again, downstairs.

The car was a Pontiac, made in U.S.A., and about as inconspicuous on the Paris streets as a battleship on the Seine. The doors were open on the sidewalk side. There was a driver already behind the wheel, and one of the muscle in the back seat. He kept a cannon trained on me as I crossed the sidewalk.

Johnny Vee was standing next to the Pontiac. His jacket was open too. He was wearing twin chest holsters.

"All the comforts of home," I said to him, nodding at the Pontiac. "Where're we going, Johnny Boy?"

"Yours to find out, punk," he answered. "Get in."

Valérie and Roscoe sat up front with the driver, Valérie in the middle. Roscoe had a deterrent at the back of his neck. Johnny's muscle held it. Johnny himself, in the middle of the back seat, held another one on me. This left Valérie unguarded, but, sandwiched as she was, she had no place to go.

We came out of the 18th Arrondissement and back onto the Périphérique. The sun had made a big try earlier in the day, but now the sky was gray again, uniformly. The air was cold, the light fading, the traffic fierce. It drove us off the Périphérique finally and onto the so-called Boulevards des Maréchaux. Before the Périphérique was built, these boulevards themselves constituted the outer rim of Paris, and though they make one long circling road, every few blocks the name changes. Ney, Soult, Poniatowski, Kellerman, Jourdan—all reminders of those nobler Napoleonic days when France used to win its share of the battles.

We made better progress on the boulevards, even with the traffic lights. Then, somewhere near the Bois de Vincennes, Valérie started working on Johnny Vee.

I'd already felt the tension building in him. Maybe he was a general, newly appointed, in the hierarchy of the mob, but right then in the Pontiac, weaving through Paris traffic on unfamiliar streets, he was no better off than a G.I. in No Man's Land. Any minute the bugles were going to blow, the booby-traps explode, and Johnny Vee was going to have to execute without thinking. His adrenalin was up, his concentration narrowed. At times like that, you don't want to think, much less talk, and the last thing you want is to be rattled.

So Valérie set about rattling him.

"What do you think, Cage?" she started in from the front seat. "Where do you think we're going?" Then, when I didn't answer right off: "Why do you think Johnny Boy doesn't want to tell us? It's pretty obvious to me, isn't it to you?"

"I think we're going to Dédé's," I said, joining in. "The scenic southern route."

"That's what I think too. I think all six of us are going to pay Dédé a visit. And Johnny Boy's going to try to trade us in exchange for a cease-fire. Isn't that the idea, Johnny Boy?"

Johnny Vee said nothing.

"You sold out on Dédé, didn't you, Johnny?" she went on. "What's the matter, cat got your tongue?"

"Shut up," he said. "Shut your cunt's mouth."

"If you ask me, Cage," Valérie said, "they're scared to death of Dédé. Dédé's in a killing mood. That's why Loulou had to call for help, all the way to California. But Johnny Boy doesn't know what he's gotten into, do you, Johnny? This is Paris, not Hollywood. You may have picked the wrong side. If you ask me, Johnny, you'd better try a cease-fire."

"Shut her up, Cage," said Johnny Vee hoarsely. "Tell her to shut her goddam yap."

"What makes you think I can shut her up?" I said.

"Because it's thanks to her, punk, that you're still alive," he blurted through his teeth. "If it was up to me, you'd never have gotten out of Amsterdam."

An illogical answer to the question, but what do you know?

I caught Valérie's eyes searching for mine in the rearview. We locked in.

"How do you figure that one out, Val?" I asked her.

"It's easy," she said, her eyes crinkling at the corners. "It's because of my father. Maître Merchadier, have you heard the name, Johnny? They told you about him, didn't they? One of the most powerful men in France. Let me tell you, Johnny, if anything happens to me, he'll never let you out of Paris alive. He'll have your private parts cut off and served with the hors d'oeuvres. You'd better believe that."

How much of what she said was truth and how much bravado I couldn't say. It had a certain logic to it, though. In the carnage at hand, the mob could have disposed of me and Roscoe with relative impunity. But maybe not Valérie.

In any case, she'd read his mentality right on the button.

I could see his jaws working out of the corner of my eye. He jammed his gun into my ribs, at the same time yelling at the muscle next to him to shut her up.

The muscle shifted his gun from Roscoe, but for a minute it was like he didn't know what he was supposed to do with it.

This left Roscoe momentarily free, and my body stiffened in anticipation. *Let's do it, man!* I shouted at him in my mind. *Grab the fucking gun!*

Only Roscoe wasn't grabbing anything.

He sat there, gray-faced. Like he hadn't heard.

When I glanced back at the rearview, Valérie's eyes were gone. They stayed gone. We went over the river and, still keeping to the boulevards, circled across the Left Bank. The traffic thinned some. We crossed the Avenue de la Porte d'Italie and stopped for a red light.

Johnny Vee told the driver to get us moving. The driver told him about the red light, in approximate English. Johnny Vee told him to fuck the red light. The driver shrugged, and with a jerk the Pontiac burst across the intersection.

Where was the goddam Law? I wondered.

But then, suddenly, it was too late for the Law.

Too late for Roscoe too, and Valérie's needle.

At the top of the Parc Montsouris, we pulled in to the curb. A man was waiting for us on the sidewalk in front of the Métro building that sits on top of the Cité Universitaire station. He had his hands in the pockets of his raincoat. He walked around in front of the car, and the driver hit the button that rolled down his window.

"You're behind schedule," the man said in French.

The driver answered him in French. It was the traffic, he explained. They exchanged a few more words, then the man stood out in the traffic, blocking it, and waved us through.

"What did he say?" Johnny Vee asked tensely.

"He said we are behind schedule," the driver answered. "Everything is in place. We can go right ahead."

We rolled up to the end of the park and turned down the street that runs alongside it. Nobody was saying anything. You could feel it all right. The bugles were going to blow, a thousand bugles, and then Johnny Vee, in a strident voice that didn't sound like it belonged to him, started telling us what was about to happen.

=16=

Mention gang wars in Paris and right away the French think Chicago. It's a knee-jerk reaction, like they've seen too many reruns of *The Untouchables*. As far as Chicago goes, I've never been there and I'm in no hurry, but I doubt Al Capone ever mobilized an army, complete with weaponry, such as went into action behind us that cold fall dusk.

I've already described Didier Delatour's hideaway: a handsome, ivy-covered house on a narrow, cobbled street of ivy-covered houses, with a back garden surrounded by a spiked fence that let out on another similar street. The area it's in forms a roughly triangular wedge, bounded by the Parc Montsouris, the Montsouris reservoir, and the big University of Paris hospital. By the time we got there, every exit hole had been plugged except ours. The Pontiac took care of that one all by itself, but just to make sure, there were two cars that pulled out from the curb behind us and blocked off the street once we'd turned in. There was just no way Delatour was going to get out alive, short of tunneling through to China.

The tactical problem was how the attackers were going to get in. Quickly and painlessly. A Paris house is built to resist intrusion. There are metal shutters that go across the windows, the walls are of stone or brick, the front doors are barricaded with various ingenious and allegedly burglar-proof devices. Nor was Dédé Delatour the type, given the circumstances, to play knock-knock-who's-there.

This was where Johnny Vee's "solution" came in.

It mayn't have been much of a plan, and I never did learn what he thought would happen if the first half of it worked. But it did have a certain element of surprise.

The surprise, very simply, was us.

Whereas if it failed, well, I guess that was part of the solution.

"You're taking us in, punk," said Johnny Vee. "The three of you. You're gonna get out of the car, you and the cunt and Cleever, you're gonna walk up to the front door, you're gonna ring the fucking bell."

"Suppose nobody's home." I said.

"Don't worry about that, wise guy. And don't try to pull anything. There'll be enough guns behind you to kill you ten times over. You walk up there and you ring the fucking bell. You try to pull anything and you're dead. Now let's go."

We were rolling slowly up the street. I remember thinking: What happens when they open the door? Maybe I even said it. I didn't have to, though. If and when the door opened, all hell would break loose. It would be every man for himself, the bugles blowing and the artillery blazing, and three people I knew were going to get caught in the crossfire. So why not at least make it four?

By this time we'd pulled up in front of the house.

"Get out!" said Johnny Vee. "You, Cleever, you and the cunt! Out! You walk around the front of the car, nice and easy." Then, to the muscle next to him: "Get out and cover them."

The two side doors opened. Roscoe got out, without resistance. And Valérie, and the muscle behind them.

"Now your turn, punk. Out! Nice and easy. Then wait for them. Then go ring the fucking bell."

I opened the door, ducked my head, and stepped out onto the

curb. The house was dark, the shutters drawn. It was so quiet you could have heard Aznavour singing at the Olympia.

If Aznavour was singing at the Olympia.

I glimpsed Roscoe and Valérie coming around the hood of the Pontiac. Presumably the muscle was crouched by the fender behind them. Presumably there were others hidden in the shadows across the street, behind the parked cars. But I couldn't see them.

I turned, ducking my head back into the car.

"What're you, chickenshit, Johnny?" I said. "Aren't you coming with us?"

Maybe it was the taunt, maybe it was Valérie's needling, maybe he'd always had it in his plan. I'll never know. But he came out then. Oh, he came out all right, but too fast, ducking his head, gun arm first.

I grabbed his arm and pulled with all my force, shouting, "GET DOWN! GET DOWN!" at the others.

I heard him curse. He tripped, his body came lunging forward, and I swung from the heels.

It had been a long time since I'd hit anybody as hard as I could. It felt good. Hell, it felt sensational! I was still shouting "GET DOWN!" and he skittered on the sidewalk and his body did a kind of crazy, arched catwalk bodies aren't made to do, and it tees me off, even now, to have to admit I had help.

The help could have come from the house or from across the street; it could even have been aimed at me. But I heard the crack of it, sharp like the snap of a whip, and it caught Johnny Vee smack in the crosshairs.

Somebody, somewhere, had panicked and pulled the trigger. Johnny Vee went down. And if there were no bugles, that was all the signal anybody needed.

—163—

I heard the shutters bang above me. I dove for cover. I hit cement hard and tried to crawl into it, and when I ran out of cement, I crawled into dirt, into plants, ivy, into brick, anywhere. Because by then the very roof of the world was falling on my head.

There was somebody home all right. When that single shot cracked out, the whole building came alive in a firestorm as quick and lethal as World War III, like the house itself was one multi-barreled gun trained on the street and pouring down a hail of lead on anything and everything, animate, inanimate, living, dead.

At first, once Johnny's "surprise" had blown, they had the edge too. The fire field was theirs, also the protection of the house, while the attackers in the street were pinned down behind improvised cover and forced to shoot uphill into a rain of terror. Their advantage, though, was short-lived. When equalized it was that Dédé Delatour was a fixed and immobilized target, attacked from the rear as well as the front. And what made it unequal was that Leduc's hybrid battalions had weapons you can't buy at your corner gun shop.

Grenade launchers, for one.

I hadn't been around live grenades in a long time, not, in fact, since that other war I've referred to, the forgotten Big K, where everybody who could bugged out, and everybody who couldn't shit his pants. I'd as soon not remember it. Suffice it that my instinct was the same: to burrow, to dig, digging into dirt and brick with my hands, feet, body, teeth, digging like a crazy mole. Because every time I lifted my head out of the muck, it was like the building, the street, the whole nutty world was shaking and cracking like a Jell-o mold caught in an earthquake.

Nowadays they go in for some pretty sophisticated varieties: "offensive" grenades, and "defensive," and grenades that only blind and deafen. These, though, were just the old-fashioned killing kind, and a couple of them bounced off the façade of the house and exploded in the street behind me. The world shook, all right, and I felt the heat when a car went up in flames. But some of them got inside through the windows, and when they went off, in a series of sucking, ear-splitting implosions, World War III, from a strategic point of view, was as good as over.

I wasn't there to see Delatour and a couple of others try to fight their way out through the stone statuary in the back garden, and I wasn't there later when the Law tried to count the holes in their bodies. What I did see, though, like marionettes in some flickering dream, was grown men running out the front door and being gunned down before they got to the sidewalk. And even one, his hands above his head and shouting, who was held upright for what seemed a long last lifetime by bullets stitching his body.

The battle had become a pigeon shoot, sickening and deadly, and what was amazing about it was that one of them managed to get through.

I saw him do it.

He came through the doorway in a low, wisplike trajectory and flung himself into the shadows, to where your hero was getting up into a dazed crouch. He was more shadow than human, a little wimp of a shadow, and somehow the bullets missed. He was making an awful throat sound, caught between a whimper and a keening. He had his cutlery in his fist, ready to rip at the first human object he met. And the first human object was me.

I've talked about self-preservation. I believe in it more than I do in heroics. I'd rather talk than fight, rather duck, rather dig, and this for the simple reason that, nine times out of ten, the medals got awarded posthumously. But there are moments, thankfully rare, when talking, ducking, digging do you no good. When the cornered rat brings out the cornered rat.

Jeannot sprang at me. He got in one good swipe. It came from the bottom, and he aimed it low, and if I'd been standing still, he'd have opened me up from groin to chin. At that I heard a ripping sound, but if part of the rip was my own skin, I hardly noticed. Because by then I had his neck in a lock; that was what I wanted. He slipped, and I slipped with him. He was strong for his size, as slippery as he was strong, and he slashed with the knife, and a couple of times he must have struck home, but that didn't matter either. I had his neck. It wasn't judo or kung fu; if you've got to give it a name, call it the old Yakima grapple, but it was what I wanted. And I squeezed with everything I had, squeezed with a guttural, dam-bursting emotion that was close to joy. And by and by the knife dropped out of his hand.

When I let him go, he slipped out of my arms like a bag of stones.

Jesus.

That was a first for me.

Around here is where everything gets blurry. Somebody was roaring close by—a god-awful sound—and it took me a while to realize it was me. In the street the Pontiac was burning like a torch, and somebody somewhere was shouting my name. That was Valérie, but by logic that could only have come later. Because I also heard sirens, all at once and all around, WA-WOO-WA WA-WOO-WA like they make them in France, and suddenly from out of nowhere there were men running up the street, a helmeted horde of them, with padded vests and faces shielded in plexiglass, and gas bombs exploding and rifles cracking again, and when I said before that the war was over, I was dead wrong.

All I can do now, though, is try to put it down in its logical sequence.

It was the Law, of course. They were late, and no matter how they managed to gum it over in the subsequent investigations, they could only have been late on purpose. It had to be. You just don't organize and deploy a force like that in two minutes. In addition to the Police Judiciaire and the Anti-Gang Brigade there were C.R.S. too, the Compagnie Républicaine de Sécurité, those para-military para-police shock troops the state calls out on the great occasions, like when the students riot or the peasants start flinging cow pies at the Elysée Palace. In other words, Leduc's battalions were to be caught in turn, the trappers trapped, but only after their dirty work was done, and no, Virginia, there was no way it could have happened so neatly without it having been planned.

It couldn't have been just Nico's doing either. The press made a big deal out of him later—"Nicolas van den Luyken, the Netherlands aristocrat"—and to hear them tell it, it was the Dutch boy and the dikes all over again. For Nico, it turned out, hadn't stopped at Frèrejean. He'd also called the Dutch Law, and then he'd called enough people in the hierarchy of the Dutch government to make sure the Law did its job. For all I know, he also called the Secretary General at the U.N. The result, anyway, was an immediate and full-scale investigation by the Amsterdam police, who shared their findings with their French colleagues, who, reacting with superhuman zeal and alacrity, arrived at the Parc Montsouris in time to hand Organized Crime its biggest setback since Eliot Ness put in for retirement.

Sic.

All in all, it made a nice story, with a big international angle. The nicer because they managed to make it stick.

But I had another version, even though I never could have proved it. It was in what Bobet had said. It was in the way the Law lost interest in the Grimes murder once Roscoe was cleared; in the way the Atherton story had been "leaked" to the press; in the fact that the Law had showed late at the Place Clichy shoot-out. There are times when the Law always shows late, the more so in a society run by influence, and, looked at this way, it was pretty clear that Bobet had been working us, me and Valérie and Roscoe, as surely as if we'd been on his payroll. In other words, from the Law's point of view it was a case of "Got it, bear! Got it, dog!" and we'll come in to mop up the blood and win the gold stars.

Ugly if you like, but highly efficient when you're short-handed.

Let's take it back, then, to the scene in the street. I remember standing in the shadows of Delatour's house, dazed and disoriented, staring at flames and thinking somebody was calling my name. Then, without any transition, there were lights flashing all over the place and whistles, sirens, and bombs sputtering and hissing in the gutters and men charging through the swirls of smoke with rifles at the ready and plexiglass shields over their faces. I could hear the beating blades of a helicopter, and already, like no time had passed, Leduc's men were coming out of their hiding places, those that could stand or stagger, and choking, puking, their hands over their heads and a lot of years in front of them to recover from the shock. I was amazed that so many of them were still alive. It was like somebody had turned the lights on in the theater before the curtain, and if the gas played havoc among the innocent people in the neighborhood, at least they would live to tell their grandchildren about it. I stood there, transfixed, taking it in without realizing what was happening. But it was a fine performance—the best—and if it had taken the Law the better part of that day to set it up, they had the street cleaned out in a matter of minutes.

Except that they missed one man.

Valérie was shouting at me all right.

"Cage! For God's sake, *stop* him!"

I saw her then, standing in the middle of the gutter. The smoke half-enveloped her and tears streamed from her eyes. She had one hand over her face and the other extended, pointing. She too was choking from the gas, but I caught her message.

Roscoe Hadley, incredibly, was on his feet, alive and running.

For a second I simply watched him. I saw him hurdle the hood of a car and, dodging, weaving, charge down the center of the street toward the swiveling blue lights and the crowd of police waiting at the bottom.

Then I took off after him.

=17=

I ran through the smoke, choking as I went. I remember the surreal mix-up at the bottom of the street: the jam of vehicles, the flashing blue lights, the jumble of guns and helmets and walkie-talkies, the C.R.S. packed in tight like a phalanx. They grow them big in the C.R.S. and they arm them to the teeth, and when this wild-haired Watusi came charging at them, all they had to do was hit him low, hit him high, and carry him off on their shields.

But they didn't.

He went through them like Julius Erving on the front end of a fast break, and nobody laid a hand on him. He dodged across the street that was jammed up with cars and men, and when he hit the spiked fence that borders the Parc Montsouris, he put one hand on the top railing and vaulted.

By then they'd seen him all right. One of them had a revolver out and pointed when I ran past.

"God Almighty, don't shoot!" I shouted at him in the din.

Maybe he heard, maybe he didn't. Somebody else was shouting, "Make way for the ambulances!" But there were more guns than one, and they hadn't all had the chance to use them, and when Roscoe soared over the fence, a whole fusillade of bullets followed him. And one of them winged him. At least one.

I saw him go down. He fell in a clump on the other side of the fence. But almost immediately he was up again, and running, and he disappeared into the darkness.

And I went after him. For Christ's sake, don't ask me now why I did it. When I went over the fence, I heard the bullets zinging past, but none of them struck home. Then I was down, and the impact sent a shock of pain up my side, and then I was up too, and pounding through the trees under the black sky.

They close the Paris parks at sundown. The custodians make a last sweep, put everybody out, then lock the gates till morning. Maybe there are bums and kids who venture in after dark, hurdling the fences, but the Parc Montsouris, the way I remember it that night, was totally deserted. Nothing but the shadows of the trees, and somewhere some lamps were glowing faintly, and behind me the noise of the battlefield.

And somewhere, up in front, Roscoe Hadley on one wing.

I came panting out of the trees and sprinted across a wide expanse of meadow. Off to the right was the ghostly shape of the old observatory. Then more trees and out onto a path than ran uphill, between a children's playground on one side and a darkened kiosk.

Somewhere on that upslope, though, I had to slow to a trot. Then a walk. I was sweating like a pig. Every time I inhaled, pain cut through my side, and my shirt felt glued to the skin. It was like Jeannot's knife had pierced into my lungs and twisted when I breathed.

At the top of that hill, the path went across a small bridge. It gave you the impression of ending on the far side, where there was a stone parapet. Beyond the parapet, the terrain dropped off sharply.

I stopped. I held on to the bridge railing, trying to squeeze off the pain.

Then I spotted him.

I've mentioned the Ligne de Sceaux, or Sceaux Line, before. Sceaux is a suburban town to the south of Paris. An old railroad line runs out in that direction, and nowadays it extends beyond Sceaux all the way to the valley of the Chevreuse. They've long since integrated it into the Paris Métro system, but the tracks still cross the park through an open gully, then tunnel back underground after the Cité Universitaire station.

The footbridge I was standing on crossed over the tracks just at the beginning of the station. Down below stretched the platforms on either side, outbound to suburbia on the right, inbound to Paris on the left. Half-roofs slanted over the platforms, but the tracks were open, some ten meters down. Apparently he'd gone over the bridge balustrade and jumped onto the roof over the inbound platform. That part wasn't much of a drop. He was hunkered in the shadows like an animal, not far from where I stood, and cradling one arm.

Maybe he thought that was as good a place to hide as any. Maybe he was just taking five while he decided what to do next. It was hard to tell, and he wasn't telling.

We stared at each other.

"It's all over, man," I said from the balustrade. "You've got nothing to worry about any more. The bad guys have shot each other to pieces, the good guys are about to become heroes. It's time to make a deal, Roscoe."

He didn't answer. He just looked at me out of the dark.

"You've taken a bullet in your shoulder," I said. "In case you don't know, bullets that stay in the body have a way of festering soon enough. That's how you get gangrene. It's got to come out, the sooner the better."

Something broke my concentration then. I thought it was behind me, but when I turned to my right, I could see lights bobbing through the trees at the base of the slope. The Law, I thought. From where he was crouched, Roscoe couldn't have seen, but maybe he sensed them coming.

Or something else.

He tensed in the shadows.

It was time to go get him, I decided. While the getting was good.

I swung my legs over the balustrade and dropped onto the roof. At the same time Roscoe rose and short-stepped out to the edge. At the same time the noise that had distracted me, more hum than noise, took form in my brain. There was a train coming up the gully, outbound from Paris.

Roscoe turned his head toward me. For once I could read his mind.

I clambered to my feet.

"Fuck it, man!" I called out to him. "If you're going to run, I'll help you! But not that way! You'll get killed!"

Kneeling, he took the lip of the roof in his hands, then let his body swing out over the tracks. One hand lost its grip almost immediately. He held on by the other, and I heard him grunt with the effort, but then I couldn't hear anything except the train coming in a rush.

I had a moment of panic when I reached blindly for him, but then the panic broke in a brainstorm of relief. The train was *outbound* all right! That meant it was coming on the far side, away from us! That meant the worst it would do was spit dust in his face.

THEN JUMP, YOU FUCKER! my mind shouted at him. JUMP! RUN LIKE A THIEF!

I was almost on top of him when he let go.

The train reached the station. It came under me with a whoosh, and I felt the roof vibrating up into my knees.
But it wasn't stopping.
(Why the fuck wasn't it stopping?)
And it was on the wrong side, our side.
(Why was that?)
It surged through the station. Seconds later I heard a screech that never ended and the god-awful moan of an emergency horn. By then, though, incredibly, it had caught Roscoe on its front rim like a charging bull, and by the time it finished punishing his body, some hundred meters up the line, there was nothing left of him to die.

18

If I hadn't thought JUMP, he wouldn't have jumped.

Or if I hadn't chased him.

Or gone to Amsterdam. Or *Taxi Driver*. Or the Neuilly apartment. Or the St. Germain Drugstore that morning when I'd run out of tobacco.

Sure, and if pigs had wings, then we'd have to pluck feathers out of our morning bacon.

Dumb thoughts, in other words. Dangerous thoughts for somebody in my line.

Maybe that was the problem.

Fact: Even though I'd never gotten around to sending him a bill, Roscoe Hadley had been my client. Fact: I became a kind of instant hero, at his expense.

You could blame this last on the media, but the Law had a hand in it, and so did the popular taste for blood, crime, and sex. So, in her way, did my self-appointed partner. At the least, Valérie was used to celebrity. To judge, she also reveled in it, and the pictures they ran of her, in black, at Roscoe's funeral, were nothing short of stunning.

I missed the funeral. I watched it instead on the 8 O'Clock News, from a hospital bed. They made a hell of a couple, Valérie, live, and Roscoe, dead, and to heighten the poignancy, there were film clips of the mopping up at the Parc Montsouris. I saw Bobet too, and Frèrejean, and their boss, the Minister of the Interior, pushing his way between them to make sure the credit went where it was due. I even saw myself, in the hospital bed, naked to the waist except for bandages, and the newscaster was saying something like: "This intrepid American killed with his bare hands the killer who did this to him."

Blood, crime, and sex, and they did it up big. Well, it had been a long time since the Paris Law had won such a clear-cut victory against the forces of evil. Or so it could be made to appear. Killjoy that I am, I didn't think the "organized dope trade in France" had been dealt a death blow. At least not a permanent one. Too many farmers in this happy-dust world of ours count on the poppy for their cash crop, and like all it takes to start a "travel agency" is a telephone and a little protection. I even said as much to the interviewer who came with the cameras, but, needless to say, they cut my spoken parts on TV.

Rather than plead squeamishness, let me simply say that I switched off.

Or tried to.

In this respect, though, Parisians are no different from anybody else. All you've got to do is get your picture on the tube and it doesn't matter what you've done, even if you've fucked up. In other words, a lot of people that season suddenly needed a private investigator, or thought they did, or just wanted to see what one looked and sounded like. Once I got out of the hospital, my phone didn't stop ringing. The mail brought dinner invitations from people I'd never heard of, total strangers were coming up to me on the street, and finally the only way to beat it was to skip town.

Before I left, I took a ride on the Ligne de Sceaux. At odd insomniac moments, I'd been beset by this weird notion that it hadn't happened the way I've told it. My eyes had lied, the media had lied—a collective delusion. The train had stopped in time; else it had come in on the righthand track. In reality, Roscoe had dropped out of sight that night, had gotten away, disappeared, and to find a trace of him, you'd have to go off into the future to some obscure country that hasn't even been invented yet, where they'd just be starting to take up the game with the round ball and the hoop, and where there'd be rumors of a black giant with hands like scoops who was tearing the league apart.

The pigs-have-wings syndrome, call it.

I got on at the Gare de Luxembourg and rode out as far as Sceaux. The train I took did stop at Cité Universitaire. Not all did, though, as I found out. Only every other one, in fact. The ones that went all the way out to St. Rémy-les-Chevreuse, some thirty kilometers from the city, skipped the less important stations.

Like Cité Universitaire. Like the train that night when Roscoe was hanging by one hand.

The other half of the explanation—why did the Ligne de Sceaux trains drive left, when the rest of the Métro drove right?—I got from a controller who was checking tickets on the platform when I got off.

"C'étaient les Anglais, Monsieur," he told me.

I had to smile, in spite of myself. Whenever there's an anomaly in France, you can be sure the French will find somebody else to blame for it.

I asked him what the English had had to do with it, and he was happy enough to oblige. Before it was incorporated into the Métro, the Ligne de Sceaux had been an independent railroad. Like all French railroads to this day, the trains ran on the lefthand side. After all, he said, locomotion on rails was an English invention; therefore, when the first railroads came to the continent, French capital had been unwilling to invest in them. A question of politics, he said. So it was the English who put up the money and planned and built the lines, and quite naturally they did it *à l'anglaise.*

The controller talked of these events casually, like they'd happened last year. Whereas, I realized, it all went back to the middle of the nineteenth century. By that logic, you could say Roscoe Hadley had gotten his body crushed because of the Battle of Waterloo.

"But isn't it dangerous?" I asked the controller. "I mean, when the Métro runs the other way?"

"Dangerous?" he said. "But certainly! A man was killed just the other night. A black man."

"So I heard. Then isn't it time you changed over?"

"Ah, that," he said. "That, Monsieur, is out of my hands."

I went by plane.

I went alone too, pulling a Roscoe.

The Riviera, you'll hear, isn't what it used to be. The air is polluted, the water too, and the prices are outrageous, and there are too many Germans. (Or English, Americans, Belgians, Dutch, pick one.) But if you hit it between seasons, when it's too cold to swim and you can walk into the good restaurants without having reserved a week in advance, it's still a pretty good place to get away from it all. In case of bad weather, bring along a girl. If you forget, though, chances are you'll find one on the spot.

That's what I did. Her name was Janine, and I found her sitting in the Negresco bar. Sure enough, she worked for Air France when she wasn't on vacation, and we knew some people in common.

One thing led to another thing, and without my having planned it that way, my rest turned into a "warrior's rest," which is the French way of saying R-and-R. We spent the rainy days in bed, Janine and I, and parts of the bright ones too. An uncomplicated relationship, and once it happened, I figured it was just what I needed. We walked the deserted beaches, weather permitting, and toured the fortified hill towns of the back country. At night we made the casinos. A gang of elegant Kuwaitis was monopolizing the action that season. They came to play in Rollses, and clipped their cigars with cutters sprinkled with diamonds, and got clipped in turn, and felt no pain.

Neither did I.

Still...

According to Janine, it wasn't Roscoe Hadley. It was the girl, what was her name?

"You mean Valérie?" I said.

"*Oui, celle-là.*"

"Forget about Valérie," I told her.

"I can, *chéri*," she said. "But what about you?"

I thought I could. Hell, I thought I had.

By way of testing our respective theories, I even took her to a basketball game. Several of the French pro teams play on the Riviera. One of them had had its American players implicated in the scandal and its opponent's that night had been temporarily suspended, along with all foreign pros playing in France. This at least kept the league from turning into a farce, and maybe it convinced the fans the sport really was being cleaned up.

Anyway, the match-up we saw was held in a pretty little

bandbox that would have fit into a corner of the Forum in L.A., and played that way, by home-bred Frenchies with a lot of enthusiasm and doubtful talent, the game had something quaint about it. It took me a long way back, to the late forties, when basketball still belonged to the little guys and such giants as there were were too clumsy to do more than block the lane. The tactics, this night on the Riviera, were either run-and-shoot or bob-and-weave, with a slight preference for bob-and-weave. Every so often the ball would go in to the big guy at the post. He'd either drop it or get fouled as he turned to shoot. He'd miss his foul shots and then the cavalry charge would start back in the other direction. If you were seeing it for the first time, it looked like fun, and not only fun but accessible. You could hear the players shouting at each other, the slap of rubber on hardwood, and I imagine some of the younger spectators in the crowd felt like putting on their sneakers and joining in. But I wasn't seeing it for the first time, and when we got up to go, midway through the second half, we weren't the only ones.

The Americans would be back all right. If not Roscoe Hadley, then a bunch of black leapers who would make us fans forget Roscoe Hadley.

Which is precisely what did happen. Though where they came from or who sent them I've no idea, and I never tried to find out.

R.I.P.

=19=

The phone call came from an unexpected source. It was an officer at the American Consulate in Nice. He wanted to talk to me about an urgent, if at the same time rather delicate, matter.

I wanted to know how he'd found me.

It was the Embassy in Paris, he said. He was only acting as messenger.

I wanted to know how the Embassy in Paris had found me.

That he didn't know.

The next morning, in any case, I went around to the Consulate, a classy joint just off the Promenade des Anglais, and met the officer in question. He turned out to be a tall, gawky Midwesterner, affable enough, with a State Department veneer and just a hint of C.I.A. He explained the situation, as he understood it. Of course he couldn't judge the rights and wrongs, and his counterpart in Paris couldn't either. However, his counterpart in Paris hoped that it could be worked out amicably, and soonest, without the intervention of the French authorities. Otherwise it could prove most embarrassing, not only for the Embassy but for me as well.

We put through a trunk call to his counterpart in Paris, who told me the same thing his counterpart in Nice had. He leaned on the urgency of the matter, and I agreed to an appointment that same afternoon. In Paris, my hotel.

Maybe all I'd been waiting for was a push. Janine and I caught a midday Air Inter flight, and we landed at Orly an hour later. The sun was already low in the sky as we rode into town and it wouldn't get much higher till spring, but the city had a cold, sharp, end-of-year beauty to it, and I could smell its tang even with the windows of the cab rolled up. I kissed Janine goodbye outside her pad in Montparnasse. She said it had been great. I promised to call her. Then I rode alone down the rue d'Assas, glomming the traffic and the shopwindows.

I'd just gotten to my suite and was starting to thumb through the accumulated mail when the two of them came up. I never did catch the name of the man from the Embassy. The other, though, was Mr. Robert Richard Goldstein, book publisher, of New York, New York.

As a friend of mine once said of somebody else, probably the only trouble with Bobby R. was that he wore his shirt collars too tight. Otherwise, he was nattily dressed and highly self-important. I put him well within cardiac range, and when he blew his top, which, to judge, was often, he went purple from the shirt collar up. He made a big deal about all the trouble his goddam son had caused him, but it turned out he'd come as far as London on business, and Paris is only an hour away.

He'd brought along the Embassy man as witness. He was fed up, was Bobby R. Fed up with being fucked around by two-bit investigators. He was going to have me disbarred, locked up, deported, my license torn up in little pieces and thrown down the goddam toilet. He didn't know how things worked in France, but it was a civilized country, he was sure they had laws on fraud and embezzlement, he was going the goddam limit with me. By the time he was finished with me, I was going to wish I'd never heard of Bob Goldstein.

The Embassy man wore that can't-we-settle-this-amicably expression of his breed, but the more Bobby R. blew, the less sure he seemed of it. Clearly, though, he'd already decided which one of us had more clout.

As for me, I let this literary Vesuvius have his day. Then, when he was done, I said: "Why?"

"Why what?" said Bobby R. The purple of his face had begun to break up into splotches.

"Why do you want to do all those terrible things to me?"

"I told you," he said. "I'm sick and tired of being fucked around."

"Fucked around?" I said. "I'm sorry, Mr. Goldstein, but I don't see it that way. Not at all. From where I see it, I've fulfilled my end of the bargain."

"You've *what?*"

The purple came back and the cords in his neck bulged against the collar.

"That's right," I said. "Look at it my way. You paid me a month's retainer to find your son, correct? I didn't find him in a month, so we renewed for a second month. All right, so I found him. I told you that, the last time we talked on the phone. I also told you your son didn't want any part of you. I believe he told you the same thing himself. Maybe that's a sign of sickness on his part, maybe it's filial ingratitude, I wouldn't know. But I'm not a wet-nurse, and I don't run a lock-up for wayward youth, and if that's what you want, you'll have to find it elsewhere."

"I sent you a check, you bastard! What are you trying to pull? You can't quit now, I sent you another check!"

"I don't know anything about another check," I said.

"Do you see what I mean?" he bellowed at the Embassy man. "I told you he was a fucking crook!"

"Now wait a minute," I said. "Just hold everything. I've been out of town for a while, I haven't even opened my mail. If you'll just keep the lid on a second, I'll take a look."

I picked up the stack and started through it again. Sure enough, there was an envelope from his publishing house in New York. I opened it. There was a letter inside, also a check. The check, it turned out, was made out for the same figures Bobby H. had laid on me that night in the kitchen. Only they had a dollar sign in front of them.

I stuck the check into the letter, then folded the letter back into the envelope and held it out to him.

"I'm sorry," I said, "but I can't accept this."

"What do you mean, you can't accept it? You can't back out now, it's too late for that. A deal's a deal!"

"There is no deal," I said. "I make it a rule never to work for two clients in the same family. You'll have to go to somebody else."

It was cardiac time all right.

"What was that you said?"

"Just what I said," I answered. "Since the last time we talked, your son's hired me himself."

"For Christ's sake! What the hell for?"

"To keep you off his back, Mr. Goldstein."

Probably I shouldn't have said that. I mean, probably there's a law somewhere in the Napoleonic Code against inducing apoplexy in susceptible individuals. Bobby R. went through purple into a dangerous shade of blue. He was used to having his way, and to browbeating the people who worked for him till he did. But I didn't work for him any more, and though I held no brief for Bobby H., I'd seen enough of Daddy to feel something approaching sympathy for him.

We might have ended up in fisticuffs, or pistols at dawn, or God knows what, if there hadn't been a knock at the door.

"*Entrez!*" I called out, thinking it was the hotel staff.

It wasn't, though.

I saw the expression on Bobby R.'s face change in mid-expletive. I turned myself and saw them, and the surprise of it brought a grin to my face, one I couldn't suppress entirely.

She'd set it up all right. It had to be. The timing was too perfect. She'd set us all up.

Resourceful bitch.

Valérie and Bobby H. walked into my sitting room. She'd abandoned black, I noticed, for something more everyday, but the aura of chic and sexiness was still intact. Bobby H., on the other hand, was wearing one of those half-smiling, half-contrite expressions prodigal sons put on for the great reunions. I only found out the reason for it later. Apparently his dreams of free and glorious enterprise had gone up like so much hash. The Dutch connection had broken down; a couple of his "distributors" had been picked up by the Law. Another day and Bobby H. might have found himself where even Daddy would have had trouble helping him.

"Keep it, Cage," said Valérie.

"Keep what?"

"There's a check in that envelope, isn't there? Keep it. We earned it."

I noticed the *we*.

I looked at the envelope, then at the publisher, but he only had eyes for the product of his masculinity. The Embassy man had crossed his legs and was making a show of examining his fingernails.

"Come on, Cage," said Valérie, taking the envelope from my hand. "We've got things to do."

She stuck the envelope in my pocket, took my arm, and we left them. I don't think they noticed.

We walked toward where I'd left the Giulia a few short centuries ago. The streetlights were already on. The windshield of the Giulia was plastered over with parking tickets, and it was only an act of God that they hadn't towed it away.

"You set it all up, didn't you?" I said. "Including the meeting upstairs?"

"I thought you'd been gone long enough," was all she answered.

I started to ask her how she'd found me, but I knew what her response would be: secrets of the profession.

"Well," I said, "it looks like I'm in your hands. What happens now?"

"Have you forgotten? That day on the road? You called it a beautiful idea."

"No, I haven't forgotten. But there were two beautiful ideas."

"But only one of them mattered," she said.

I remembered all right. I kissed her for openers, next to the Giulia. I could feel the grin spreading again inside me, and it met no obstacles.

Only then it did.

I was feeling around in my pockets.

"Shit," I said. "The car keys. I must have left them upstairs."

I turned to go back, but she held on to me.

"Wait a minute, Cage," she said.

The dimples had creased at the corners of her mouth. She opened her fist and dangled them at me.

"It's cold," she said. "Let's get going."

I took the keys from her, and we went.